The Zombiology World... So far

The Reset

A zombie apocalypse is here, but figuring out how to survive in the immediate aftermath is only the first step.

Elaine is just an ordinary woman, but when the apocalypse occurs, she must find a way to survive in an increasingly hostile world. Enter Liam, the policeman who saves her at their first meeting and provides assistance as they try to cope with the zombie outbreak brought about by an unknown infection that's spreading out of control.

Together they form a community, trying to save as many lives as they can, a place where people can be safe. Even in the throes of disaster though, emotions creep up, taking both of them by surprise. Who knows? They might just get their happy ever after...if they can survive.

I Dream of Zombies

After the apocalypse the world was a different place. Those who survived did so by wits, strength and by banding together.

Julia is a soldier—not by choice but circumstance in a world where taking up arms is a necessity. She's buried the softer parts of herself including her heart.

Leroy on the other hand is a warrior. An ex-soldier who has to come to terms with what he hides and a loner by choice.

Now they have a mission—retrieve those missing from *Camp Queanbeyan*. Survival is just the first step on a rocky road toward redemption and there's no guarantee of success.

Six Million Dollar Zombie

What do you get in the middle of a zombie apocalypse when you mix Canberra, a Priest and Kindergarten teacher?

Sparks. Lots of red-hot sparks of passion.

Dove may be a priest, but he's also a man and he's been alone for a long time. Rescuing Leonie by the side of the road is just the first step on a journey no one expected to love.

Leonie is running. Her family is gone, the zombies are chasing her, and she's rescued by a priest on a motorbike and taken to a community which welcomes her.

Life should only get better, but the forces who began the apocalypse are building an army of mutated, super-strong zombies. They plan to overtake everything those in the communities have built.

Times are only going to get tougher until they can defeat those with no interest in survival.

Make Room For Zombies

The Zombie Invasion—a failed government experiment—continues to spread...

When Adrienne makes the decision to pack up her infant twins, Leanne and Fiona, and make for an island, she has no idea just how much her life will change. The young widowed mother of two-month-old twins can't stay where she's been, because they're demanding more than she can give. They need her to be a warrior—something she isn't. The only option is to run to the idyllic island off the coast of Queensland.

The island might be cut off from the mainland with just one fortified bridge, but Jack knows it won't take much for the zombies to invade. With a half baked plan to blow up the bridge and the self-proclaimed mayor missing in action, he doesn't really need more responsibility.

That is until he meets Addie and the babies. Now, he's got so much more at stake than just the islanders protection. He's got a ready made family, if they can just survive the next few weeks.

Only time will tell, especially when zombies are involved.

THE RESET

A ZOMBIOLOGY NOVEL

Imogene Nix

Love Books
Publishing

PROLOGUE

Elaine's fingers curled over the radio, her heart stuttering with fright.

"Officials are unable to determine the cause of the illness breaking out all over the city, but urge calm. If you are cornered by the infected, seek safety. Should you be bitten, seek medical attention immediately."

Her fingers fluttered against her lips. The dirge rose, long moans as those infected, their skin turning a deep grayish green and their eyes milky white, howled outside the office. Elaine pushed the curtain aside once more and glanced through the glass. The collection had grown, their faces slack yet eerily aware that she remained inside.

"I don't know what to do." She turned back to watch as her boss, William Eckerman, rocked in his seat. "I mean, we've been holed up here for over two days. There's no food in the kitchenette, the toilet is overflowing, and we can't stay here, otherwise we'll die." The jitter of her stomach warned her that panic was rising up, about to overwhelm her.

"Elaine, relax. It's just a precautionary measure. The police will come and..."

"The police have indicated that they are overwhelmed. Military forces are on the way, but communications are hampered by the...by the walking dead converging on sites with power. In the latest update, the government is ceasing all non-urgent tasks. They're recommending that you hunker down and hope you can ride it out. Resources are limited, and it's suggested that, if possible, you should stock up and find a safe location in which to secure yourself." The announcer's voice shook.

"See? They're saying we need to find a secure location, stock up, and hide. Mr. Eckerman, we can't stay here." The urge to flee coursed through her veins like an exploding freight train. "We have to go to our homes. Be with our families."

He flicked invisible specks of lint from his immaculate sleeves and rocked again in the seat. "Well, Elaine, I think, given your current level of excitement, you should certainly go home."

She frowned at the cool tone. "Uhhh, Mr. Eckerman?" "Yes?"

"Mr. Eckerman—"

"When this is over, I'll give you an excellent reference for the four years of service. It's sad that something has overset you to the point where completing your work is no longer your priority. I understand it is probably time to expand your employment horizon."

As she stood there listening to the drivel he was spouting, growing anger warred with her terror. "Mr. Eckerman..."

"Go on and get your things together. It's best you go directly home."

She shuffled to her desk, shock assaulting her as she gathered the few personal items she'd stashed. The photo of her parents, the Mickey Mouse cup she'd bought at a major attraction. The hairbrush and small clutch of cosmetics joined the rest of her belongings, then Elaine straightened, turned, and headed for the door.

"Aren't you forgetting something?" Mr. Eckerman held out his hand, and she blinked. "Umm, what?"

"Keys."

She blinked again then made an 'O' with her mouth. "I forgot them when I came in. I'll have to drop them off once everything is done."

He snarled and opened the door. "Go on then. I want them back here as soon as the situation is cleared."

She looked outside, glad he'd insisted on staff using the back door, which was protected by the security fencing and remote-controlled roller door. She hurried to her vehicle, pleased it was older and heavier, sure it would protect her until she reached home.

Leaving the building was scarier than she expected. As she drove the short distance she constantly glanced around, seeing small huddles here and there of those who were infected. Each time they lurched in her direction she panted, heartrate increasing, adrenaline spiking until she was past them.

Turning onto her street left her amazed. Smoking wrecks of cars littered the street, and several gray-skinned individuals loitered. She drove carefully, hoping she could make it home without being waylaid.

When she reached her house she swung in to park on the road, thinking she'd have plenty of time to get in the house without any of the walkers in the way. She found the key for the front door, checked the rearview mirror to make sure none of the infected were close by, then got out of the car. Slamming the car door shut, she engaged the locks and sprinted to her front door.

Fighting the jamb until the door eased open, Elaine slid within and pushed the door shut. The tiny house on the outskirts of town she shared with her best friend had a deserted feel to it.

"Emily?" Once sure the door was securely latched she hurried up the hall, calling her friend's name. Every door she opened and peered inside was empty, and at the end of ten fruitless minutes she slumped down in a kitchen chair.

*** *

Liam wasn't sure what to do. The supermarket was empty, and shelves of food were scattered on the floor as he picked his way along the aisles.

"They said to lay in supplies then hunker down." He glanced at the phone in his hand. "They didn't say to break into the supermarket though." Ramon, his half-brother, snickered into the camera of the phone, and Liam shrugged.

They'd flown into Canberra three days ago and settled into the tiny B-and-B on the edge of this township. The location seemed great, only a few miles from Parliament House. It was close to the venue of the three-day conference he was attending on policing in emergency situations. Ramon had come because he'd concluded his last contract in an African country with a bubonic plague epidemic and was at a loose end.

No one could have expected something like this outbreak to occur though, and food was a priority. Liam had insisted Ramon stay at the B-and-B. Having a brother who was an epidemiologist and infection prevention specialist meant he might be called upon by the authorities for assistance, and they couldn't afford for him to be infected by the virus.

"Okay, I'll see what I can find and get back there as quickly as I can." Liam disconnected the call and turned to scan the shelves. "Long-life milk, because it will be good for at least a year on the shelf, sugar, coffee. Bottled water. Some powdered milk as well." He thrust them into the trolley and moved as quickly as he could toward the end of the aisle.

A groan stilled him. He'd already seen the results of those infected, the way they set upon victims, the dripping, bloody teeth. If that moan was anything to go by, he was no longer alone in the shop.

"Get back!" The startled words of a woman almost had him jumping.

"Hello?" He cursed inwardly for now making himself a target as the sound of shambling footsteps echoed, moving in his direction.

"He's heading your way!" the woman yelled as the gray man turned the corner, eyes blank, mouth slack through dripping trails of scarlet. The outstretched hands moved toward him. He didn't have anything on him that would be considered a weapon and cursed that decision. The paperwork for going armed in public—something the department had been cracking down on lately—would have been worth it after all.

The creature extended its arms and gave an "uhhh" sound, and he pondered for a moment whether there was some way to disable it. The thought came and went when the woman screamed and a second and third shuffler made its way in his direction.

The handle of the trolley was just in reach and he tugged it backward, braced his legs, then ran in the direction of the shuffler. The trolley hit the creature in the chest, and it went down, legs and arms waving frantically until it rolled. Now the sound that emanated from its mouth became more of a growl of fury.

He reached out, his hand curling around the nearest can. Saying a silent prayer, he aimed and threw. The crack of heavy metal on bone and the spray of blood as the man went down without a whimper gave him momentary pleasure, but not before the woman from the next aisle scurried around to him.

"There's two more," she screamed.

He didn't glance at her, merely reached up, grabbed another tomato soup can, and lobbed. It hit without the power to cease the onward march.

"Dammit!"

"I've... There's some kitchen string here. Would that help?"

He turned briefly and acknowledged the beautiful, curvy, red-haired woman thrusting the plastic-wrapped item at him, but he shook his head as they stumbled backward.

"We're going to need something a little more useful." He considered what might be here in this tiny store as the woman disappeared before returning with two long, metal-headed rakes. "What about these?" she asked.

He laughed, grabbed one out of her hands as the walkers came within reach, and thwacked it down hard on the head of the nearest one. The rake dropped with a thud and rolled under the shelving unit.

She made a sound, rather like a moan, and turned away as he snatched the other implement and used it to push the other shuffler back.

This time he lined up the male, sidestepped its attempt at grabbing him, then swung this new rake like a bat. The infected individual fell to the floor, and he brought the rake down on its head. She turned and retched while he waited.

"They're... Those were humans! Why did you—"

"No, they aren't humans anymore. They were zombies, and they'll kill you as soon as look at you. Now grab what you need so we can get out of here."

He glanced down one last time at the remains he'd left on the floor. He felt bad about what he'd had to do, but sugarcoating the truth wouldn't make it any better. The only thing they could do was stock up and get back to safety.

He threw tins and jugs into the trolley, along with frozen items, which he was sure would only be available for a little while longer. He also tossed in other essentials such as toilet rolls. He noted that the woman, tears flowing down her cheeks, followed his lead.

Then, with both trolleys full, they left the store and headed to the carpark. This was the danger time. He pulled out his cellphone and dialed Ramon. "Hey, I've got a full load and I'm heading in."

"Good, 'cause I'm hungry and the radio is just repeating what we already know."

He turned to the woman. "Will you be all right to get home?"

She sniffled inelegantly and nodded. "I'm just over the road there." She pointed to the

tiny cottage beside the B-and-B residence where he was staying, and he laughed. When she glanced at him, he sobered. "I'm right next door."

"Oh."

CHAPTER 1

They ran toward the road, the wheels of the trolleys crunching and whirring as random bits of asphalt made themselves known. Headed directly for her front door, Elaine spied something or someone from the periphery of her view. She knew the blue dress, the bright red hair. But that was where anything she knew ended. The sightless gaze of the walker had her gulping.

"You okay?" the man beside her enquired, but all she could do was shake her head.

No, I'm not okay. My best friend Emily is one of the walking undead. I'm pushing a trolley toward my front door and trying to dodge spattered bits of... With great effort, she halted the hysterical answer in her mind.

"I'll be fine." It took every ounce of willpower to answer as the bile rose up, threatening to swamp her with nausea.

His gaze zeroed in on Emily, or whatever was left of her, and he frowned. "You could come to our place." They'd almost reached the other side of the road, but she shook her head, needing time alone to regroup and settle the thrumming nerves.

"No, I'm good. But look, at the end of the garden there's a small gate between the two yards. I'll pop over later, when I'm a little more settled."

He grunted as they pushed the trolleys up the concrete lip and sprinted to the door. "Do that, or I'll be over there checking on you."

Elaine fumbled for her keys, found them, and shoved them into the lock. It turned, and she whispered a prayer of thankfulness. Shunting the door open, she moved past the trolley then pulled it up the tiny step into the house just as Emily turned the corner toward the front door.

As much as she wanted to help her friend, she'd seen exactly what she was. Dead. Or undead, though that truth was so confronting! Elaine slammed the wooden door just before Emily made it to her.

Staring at the door, Elaine heard the grunting and scratching on the wood. In her mind she could picture Emily's long nails clawing at the door. She waited for Em's familiar, 'Hey, let me in!' sure that she wasn't really dead but merely playing some stupid trick. The words didn't come. In truth, having seen Emily, or what remained of her, she guessed she hadn't really expected it, but it was so damned hard to accept.

In the narrow hallway, she slumped on the floor, breathing deeply while waiting for the adrenalin to wash away. She was thankful the heavy door lay between her and what was outside. With a sigh Elaine stood and dragged the metal trolley to the kitchen so she could empty the contents into the fridge and cabinets. The silence that now reigned was deafening, so she reached over to the tiny kitchen television and flicked it on to the cable news channel she preferred.

A harried-looking woman sat at the news anchor desk. "Government sources have informed us that the situation is deepening, while those on the street, infected or changed, have increased in numbers. You are asked to stay inside your home where it's safe. To hunker down and expect little assistance at this time from the police or armed services. Our own intelligence shows the number of infected is rising exponentially. However, we've been unable to contact any form of security forces, and the situation is grim. Please, take all care. If in danger from those who are walking, we have ascertained that any bites or scratches rapidly spread and infect those injured."

The woman reading the update stopped and shook her head, her face starkly white under the lighting.

"If you're bitten or scratched, our sources indicate that infection transferal is one hundred percent. We've seen this firsthand, and have received reports of those infected and carrying extreme injuries continuing to attack long beyond what could normally be expected."

Without thought, Elaine reached for a chair and slumped into it. "How can this be? They're talking about zombies on the news. Zombies!"

The rising tide of hysteria threatened to overwhelm her, and she had to work at controlling it, with deep, lung-cleansing breaths.

She'd get through this. "I have to." But right now, it didn't seem like an easy proposition, and tears dripped down her face.

*** *

"She's next door. Man, at least we've got each other. Mum being gone kind of makes it easier but..." Liam's voice trailed away as Ramon stared at him.

"You're talking about some woman you met in the shop, in the middle of a crisis." Liam nodded. "True, Ramon, but she's alone and next door. I mean, we could—"

"Now isn't the time to be finding a girl, Liam. We need to get our hands on a car, get into the city and see if—"

"You're wrong. This is exactly the time we should be helping others. Dammit, she's alone with no one to protect her, and that's my specialty." He couldn't help the knot of anger that swelled in his belly. Ramon might be good with diseases and illnesses, but when it came to helping others, to sorting out immediate problems, that's where Liam's abilities kicked in. "I'm going to nip around the back and see—"

"Liam!" His brother's shocked voice didn't stop him as he pushed past the cart toward the back door. "We don't know if the virus is airborne or..."

Liam shrugged. If it was, he'd already possibly been infected. He was more than prepared to take his chances to help the red-haired woman he'd met.

At his push, the glass door slid open and he stepped through into the secure backyard. The high, wooden fence ensured privacy between the two cottages, but there was a gate at the back he'd spied when they'd arrived. His feet crunched on the grass, dry after the long months without rainfall. The gate squeaked open when he turned the handle and pushed, and he shut it behind him, carefully scanning the area and noting the shady trees and a metal shed, then he headed to the back door.

When he reached the door, he knocked with three short raps.

The door opened cautiously. He frowned as he took in the woman's rumpled appearance and her red, swollen eyes. "Are you okay?"

She nodded and sniffled. "Yeah. Just watching the news and..." She ran her fingers through her disheveled hair. "Uh, come in."

Liam crossed the threshold and waited for her to close and latch the door.

"I didn't mean to interrupt, but I wanted to check on you. By the way, my name is Liam." "Mine is Elaine." The woman held out her hand, and he shook it. "Would you like a coffee?"

For a moment, the urge to laugh rose up, but he restrained it ruthlessly. "That would be lovely."

She gave him a weird look. "Umm, everything okay next door? I mean, you seemed a little out of it when I asked you about coffee." She puttered over to the stove, ignited the hob, and placed the kettle on the flame.

He gave a half-bark of laughter. "It just feels so damned normal, you know? That shouldn't be odd, except nothing is normal anymore."

She nodded, spooning the crushed beans into a mug, and turned back to him, her eyes shining. "I don't know what's going to happen next. It's kind of disconcerting."

"And you've been crying," he pointed out.

"I... I saw my friend Emily as I got back to the house. She's..." She sniffled, and he understood.

"I'm sorry."

Elaine nodded, and they settled onto the large stools before the granite benchtop, waiting for the pot to boil.

"Have you lived here long?"

She nodded. "I grew up here with my grandmother. My parents died in a car accident years ago, so she raised me. And I inherited the house from her. Em moved in about eighteen months ago. Her mother had thrown her out and she needed somewhere to stay. But now..." Elaine sighed.

"Ramon and I lost Mum twelve months ago. She had cancer, but it was swift. At least she didn't have to see this." He waved his hands, knowing she'd understand. "Dad took off when we were little, and it was just us. I had a gig at a conference here and Ramon decided to join me, but clearly our timing really sucked."

She giggled. The kettle started whistling, and she slid from her chair and pulled it off the stovetop. "I know, right? But what are we supposed to do? I don't want to leave my home. It's the only one I've ever known. Gran bought it when it was first built, and Chisholm was just starting to pop. She wanted somewhere a little more quiet. She'd grown up in Sydney, and when Gramps died, she decided she really hated the traffic, the noise, and having too many people around her."

"Yeah, I understand. We decided to stay here because we were looking for the quiet too. Well, as much as you can find in Canberra."

"How do you like your coffee?"

"Sweet, two sugars and milk, thanks."

He watched as she moved around, gathering what was needed to fulfill the request. He'd never known a woman who moved with such an economy of motion, he noted she used only what she needed. Elaine immediately replaced the items no longer required back in the cupboard then pushed the cup in his direction.

"What kind of conference did you come for?"

He gave a tiny laugh. "Policing in traumatic events. Ramon came with me as he's just home from Africa where he was dealing with a minor pandemic."

Her lips formed an 'O' and his body tightened just enough to make him consider his immediate attraction. She didn't strike him as a weak, grasping female, just one totally out of her depth.

"He's an epidemiologist. Works with things like Ebola."

She shuddered but nodded.

"What do you do?" he asked.

"Not much, it would seem. My boss fired me yesterday after I insisted I needed to come

home. He runs a mail-order medical supply company. After most of the staff didn't turn up, he insisted we should stay there. But the food was running out, and the news and radio urged everyone to go home. He didn't, but I think it's more because he was afraid to spend much time with his family. He's a workaholic."

The conversation felt normal, but his brain knew there was nothing everyday about the situation. His phone buzzed, and he reached for it.

"I'm needed at the local hospital. Can you drag yourself away long enough to help me find a ride?" Ramon's discontent was clear with his curt speech, and Liam knew he was getting upset.

"Hang on." He tugged the phone away from his ear. "I don't suppose you have a car, do you?"

Elaine blinked at him. "Uh, yes?"

"Could you give us a lift to the hospital?" He'd barely finished speaking when she blanched.

"Your brother..."

"He's needed at the hospital. I guess they want his advice and assistance. Can you help us out?"

"Oh, yes. Sure. I'll go grab my keys." "Uh, where's the car?"

At that she grinned. "It's actually in the garage at the back of the yard. I moved it this morning, before there were any of the infected around." Elaine grimaced. "I didn't want to have to fight them, and the shed has an automatic door so I can be in and out without any worries of them in the yard."

"Awesome." He gulped down the rest of his coffee, ignoring the slight discomfort as the hot drink burned his mouth. "I'll go grab Ramon and his things, and we'll be back in a moment."

*** *

Once Elaine met Ramon she was fairly sure that he didn't like her. It wasn't that he was rude—instead, he was scrupulously polite—but he was cool toward her. In fact, if it wasn't for the current situation, she wasn't sure she'd want anything to do with him either. Unlike his brother. Wasn't that a kicker?

Liam was cute, personable, and somehow protective of both her and his brother. He could easily be the meat in the sandwich if she didn't get her lust in control. And she lusted him. Big time.

He was good-looking, with a healthy, golden bronze in his skin, shining green eyes, thick, wavy, blond hair, and he was built like Adonis. Totally yummy. He was also clean-shaven, which showed his beautiful jawline.

They piled into the car, Liam in the seat next to her. She ignored the tiny car beside hers. It was Emily's, and right now she didn't want to think about her friend and what had happened to her, so she put it out of her mind.

She pressed the button on the dash and waited as the garage door rose. She inched out slowly, then pressed the button again, waiting to make sure no zombies got inside the building, then pulled onto the road.

She turned left and squealed. "Oh my gosh! There's people on the street!" Her hand hovered over the garage door remote as she considered opening the door for those seeking shelter, but Liam stopped her.

"Wait. I'm not sure they're normal. Look how they're shuffling. I think they're..."

Elaine squinted and sighed. "I think you're right, but they're blocking the way, Liam. I don't want to hurt them."

A strangled sound came from the back seat. "They're infected, and from what I've been able to work out, there's no current cure. You'll need to make your way through them."

Her gut clenched. "I'm not going to run them over." Elaine couldn't control the tone of her voice and the way it rose at the end. Nausea clawed at her throat, and the burn of bile triggered tears.

Liam coughed and spluttered. "I don't think that's what Ramon means, but keep your window up and drive slowly. We'll need to pick our way through the mess, okay?"

She nodded furiously, understanding he was looking to find some kind of common ground between his brother's 'we need to get there' mentality and her 'won't hurt them' attitude. They drove slowly, zigzagging through the shuffling mass, making slow progress as she listened to Ramon's grunts of dissatisfaction.

Once they'd navigated through the avenues, they finally made it onto the main street, littered by crashed cars and strange lumps that Elaine reluctantly realized were likely human...or past human. That thought was like a stone in her belly.

"Are they... Are they dead?" Her hands shook on the steering wheel.

Elaine expected Ramon to laugh at her, but the silence was deafening.

"Liam?"

The expression on his face calmed her. "We aren't yet sure what you could call it. All we know is that it's like a virus, transmitted by a bite or scratch."

The hospital appeared before them, and she drove with a single-minded focus. At the door, Ramon cleared his throat. "You'd best head home. I'll ring once I have some more details."

Liam grunted and reached for his brother's hand as he opened the door. "Ramon? Stay safe, bro. I have no intention of losing you."

"You bet, brother. As you know, I'm not that easy to lose. Straight home with yourself. I'll ring for a lift if I can't organize something, okay?"

Ramon grabbed the bag he'd brought with him, slammed the car door, and disappeared inside the white building.

"We should head back." Her voice wobbled.

"Yeah."

Once more Elaine locked the car and accelerated away, but she could tell Liam was focused on his brother.

CHAPTER 2

*L*iam wasn't sure what it was about Elaine that tugged at him, all he knew was that he didn't feel comfortable with her being alone. It might have been the loneliness in her gray eyes, or the sad droop of her lush lips. So, when Ramon contacted him to say he wouldn't be back, Liam nipped next door to see about staying with Elaine overnight.

With a quick knock on the door, he entered the kitchen. "Elaine, I was thinking..."

His words trailed off when he spotted her cowering in a corner, a man advancing with a bat in his hand. Liam reacted instinctively, moving toward them.

"Stop where you are!"

The man swiveled, his face splitting into a snarling smile. "And who's going to make me?"

Liam tensed. "Step away from her or you'll regret it."

The man guffawed and Liam stilled, his hand sliding over the clip of his pistol against his hip. He didn't want to use it, but he would if necessary, as every protective instinct grew and swelled.

The man tugged the bat further back, taking the stance that told Liam what he planned to do as Elaine sobbed quietly. "Please go away. There's nothing here that you want."

Liam moved as the man's attention was focused on Elaine. He reached for the bat, tugged, and snarled as the man threw himself against him.

His hand fisted and thrust upward. It connected with the intruder's face with a resounding smack, the mash of skin and bone against soft flesh. The explosion reverberated through Liam's hand and up his arm.

Liam was rewarded by the man's bellow as he fell backward, releasing the bat, which clattered to the floor.

Scarlet splashed on the granite benchtops, the ripe scent of copper filling Liam's senses. "Get out. Get out now, and don't come back."

The man scrabbled on the floor, moving backward. "I'm outta here, man. I won't come back. Promise."

Liam didn't believe the man's vow that he wouldn't return, but he waited until the man had left the house before following down the hall to survey the broken front door. It hung with a drunken slant, the jamb hanging from wooden strips.

He moved closer, hearing the sounds of shufflers advancing. "Dammit."

There was a lounge chair nearby and he grabbed it and slammed it in front of the door as Elaine followed him.

"I'm so sorry. I was grabbing my flower pots from out front when he saw me. I closed the door and was locking it when he broke in."

Liam closed his eyes, counted to ten as the adrenaline washed away, then reopened them. "Do you think I'm angry with you?"

Elaine shrugged, making Liam sigh.

"I'm not angry with you. I'm cross you were in this position when you didn't do anything wrong. He tried to take advantage of you because he saw a woman on her own. That's not going to happen again. I'm going to nail the door shut for tonight, and tomorrow we can fix it properly. Plus, I think I should stay here with you and make sure Mr. Arsehole doesn't come back."

Elaine stared at him.

"Is that okay?"

She chewed on her lower lip, clearly thinking. "I don't know you, but to be honest, there's something about you that makes me want to trust you."

He grinned, feeling better about her words. "If it's any consolation, I'm a police officer, and you can ring my station if you need a recommendation."

Elaine frowned. "I don't think I'll need to do that. After all, you were here to save me when I needed you most." She raised her face to him, and his gut slammed hard at the tears shimmering in her eyes.

He frowned at her words. "Elaine, I'm not a knight in shining armor."

She laughed at that, the tinkle like chimes. "I know that. I'm not a wimp in normal circumstances, it's just I feel out of my element. I don't know what to do."

"First, we need to fix this door."

Elaine nodded and disappeared down the hall, returning with a tiny, pink bag of tools and a packet of nails. She watched his every movement as he hammered and secured the wood tight, testing it, then gave a nod of satisfaction.

When she sighed and slumped against the small entry table, he couldn't help himself and gathered her close. He savored the feel of her body nestled against his, all curves and bumps in the right places, so that her body and his flowed together. His mind fuzzed at the edges as the sparking of lust rose.

It took a second for Liam to clear his mind so he could think rationally again.

"No one could have expected what happened, and to be honest, we're all at sea here. We're waiting to see what's going to happen. I was talking to my sergeant earlier, and since there aren't any flights he suggested I hang tight. He's called in the rest of the team, so they can work without me right now."

"I'm pleased you're not going anywhere any time soon. I don't think I could manage on my own."

He held her close, felt the pounding of her heart, and inhaled her scent. Roses. He'd always liked roses. His mother had grown them in the garden before she got sick.

"It's getting late, and we should head to bed," she said.

For a moment his breathing ceased, his body tightened, and he squeezed his eyes shut. When she laughed, they popped back open.

"Okay, so that shouldn't have come out like that."

He took comfort from the embarrassment in her voice. "I know what you mean. Tell me where you want me to sleep and…"

"Uh, the lounge. I'll go grab some sheets, pillows, and so on."

She scurried away, leaving him there by himself. Liam gulped, sat down on the lounge chair, and started mentally listing all the reasons getting involved with her would be a bad thing.

He and Ramon would only be there for a short while. There was a major emergency and far too much danger to go getting emotionally entangled.

"Here we are."

His gaze roamed over her from the top of her red hair, shining with gold highlights under the downlights, down her lush body to her sensibly shod feet.

"Thanks." Rising up, he hoped like hell she couldn't detect the bulge in his pants, because he was struggling to keep his libido in check around this woman.

She shoved the items into his hands then turned to the lounge. With economical movements, she pulled the cushions out, and he noted the small handle. As she tugged, the base sprang open, revealing a full-sized sofa bed.

"I bought this a couple of years ago but rarely get to use it. Emily would have the odd friend over but usually they would…you know, stay in her room."

He slid his hand over hers, stopping the chatter, and she turned toward him, her eyes sparkling with emerald highlights. "We're both uncomfortable right now. It's okay."

The blush that stained her high cheekbones was delightful. Entrancing.

Then she moved, motion and speed obscuring his thoughts as she wrapped her arms around him, launched up, and set her mouth to his.

Soft. Warm. His brain kind of exploded as he opened his mouth to hers, and he tasted her. Woman and heat. Sweetness laced with timidity. He didn't touch her, though his body, tight from the brief interlude, screamed at him to do so when she drew away, breathing hard and her chest moving swiftly.

"I, uh…"

"Wow. That was some kiss." He had to clear his throat.

She turned away. "I'm so sorry." Mortification rolled off her in waves. "I shouldn't have… You probably have someone at home and…"

He sighed and reached for her, dragging her against his body. Everything about this felt so damned right in the middle of such a mess. "It's okay, Elaine. I'm not upset, and no, I don't have a girl at home. That's why Ramon came with me, because he'd be on his own there and I'd be on my own here."

Her shoulders slumped. "But I took advantage of you."

Liam's laugh roared in the sudden silence. "You haven't taken advantage of me. I'd just been going through the list of reasons why I shouldn't kiss you. So, we're about equal."

Elaine turned in his arms, her eyes shining with both excitement and unshed tears. "You're not tricking me, are you?"

He shook his head. "No. Not at all."

"We should make the bed." She stopped, blinked, and sighed. "I'm not normally like this. I feel like everything coming out of my mouth has some kind of intimate connotation."

He laughed. "Not at all. But we should head to bed. Today was trying, and I don't think there's going to be any kind of easy fix for tomorrow either."

They brushed aside their attraction and made up the bed, then she retreated for the night, upstairs to her bedroom. In the gloom, after the lights were turned off, he lay there, watching the play of the trees outside swaying in the moonlight.

What would tomorrow bring? Another encounter with a shuffler? Ramon working out what the cause was? One thing was for sure, he'd keep Elaine safe and close by, because the promise of something nibbled at his senses. He refused to ignore it and was still thinking as he fell asleep.

*** *

Elaine wondered how she'd face Liam. Awake since dawn, she listened to the birdsong in the trees, her window closed, after opening it and smelling the sickly-sweet smell of decay.

A large photo of her grandma hung on the wall, and she studied it, wishing the older lady was still alive so she could advise Elaine. "I don't know what to do, Grandma. I mean, there are bodies in the streets, and Emily's dead...kind of. Should I, you know, put her out of her misery?" Her gut clenched at that thought, and she immediately discounted it. She could barely kill a fly without feeling an immensity of guilt. "And Liam, he's so nice and good-looking. No guy has ever really given me the time of day, I'm plain and dull." Saying it all out loud left her more confused than ever, and she rested her head in her hands.

The sound of footsteps on the stairs had her raising her head. At the tap on the door, she tugged the quilt closer. "Come in."

The tray came before the man, made up with bowls, teapot, teacups, and napkins. Tears sprang into her eyes. It had been so long since anyone had treated her like this. Since before Gran's death.

"As I was rattling about in the cupboards making breakfast, I thought you could do with a little pampering. I hope this is okay."

It was so cute how off-kilter he appeared for a change. She grinned. "It's been a long time since anyone did something like this for me."

Liam unfurled the legs on the tray, and she shuffled over as he placed it down.

"Ramon called. He said they haven't made any headway, but some attackers tried to get in during the night and some of the patients took a turn for the worse. He's not sure what can be done right now. Said there's some talk about airlifting the medical staff to a secure location. He's refusing to go because there's work to do."

She nodded as Liam poured himself a cup of tea and sank into the boudoir chair beside her bed. It felt both cozy and right.

Elaine studied Liam. "So an epidemiologist and a police officer. Detective?"

He shrugged. "Guilty as charged."

She laughed at his joke. "Yeah, so both very good at what you do. You weren't just here as a delegate for that conference, were you?"

"No. I was a keynote speaker. Supposed to talk about major events and riots that took place on one of the islands where I was policing. I had planned to talk about the importance of precautions and planning."

She nodded. And here she was the office girl for some small and totally obscure medical supply company. "Why did you get into policing?"

"Because I've always been big on justice, making sure that everyone's rights are respected. Without a way to ensure people do the right thing, we'd have anarchy."

And yet, they'd met with both of them ransacking the local store. A bubble of laughter escaped.

"What?"

"We met in the store, and you and I were helping ourselves to food."

Liam grinned. "True. If things ever return to normal, I plan to go back and pay for what I took. It seems to me there'll be lots of people in the same boat, looking for food and water supplies, and if there's no one to pay, how will they get what they need?" His brow wrinkled. "Moreover, it's not safe to be out and about except for emergencies."

"Yeah. That's why I'd holed up at work, but my boss didn't think I should leave. When I came home, he demanded my keys and told me not to bother coming back. I've never not worked, Liam, and I'd been there for years. It's so surreal. How am I supposed to make do?"

Fear and confusion settled on her like a heavy coat until he touched her hand. "It's okay to feel scared, Elaine. It's what we do with those emotions, how we put them to good use and help others that counts right now."

She bit her lip. "I really want to, but where do we start?"

He scratched his chin and she noted the blond scruff. An emotion she'd rarely felt before—the punch of lust—hit her hard in the belly.

"I was thinking, we don't know how long this is going to go on, right? But it's a fair bet it's going to take a while. One of the things we could do, after we lay in supplies, is you need a garden. Somewhere you can gather the supplies you need. I know the weather can get cold in winter and hot in summer, but with a little bit of effort, you could be getting supplies year- round."

"So, you're expecting this to last a while?"

"To be honest, I can't see how this can be overcome in a year or two. While the shamblers are around, no one is safe. I tried ringing the agent I rented the property through and got a girl. She said the owners were fairly uninterested before all this happened, and now they're even less likely to be checking on the welfare of the property, and since we're still alive and all..." He shrugged, his words trailing off.

Elaine bit her lip. She felt the sting and tasted the coppery tang as she broke the skin.

"The news was saying that they'll be shutting down broadcasts soon. That all the non- essential parts of government had disbanded and they are telling everyone to go home, stay off the streets, find out which neighbors are still alive and help them."

"It's like a zombie apocalypse movie, except it's not a movie or nightmare, is it, Liam?"

"No."

"Emily is out there. And other people I know probably are too. What are we supposed to do?"

"I don't know right now, Elaine. I guess we stay here and try to make the best of it." She gripped the tiny, flowered teacup. "I have seeds, and there's a greenhouse Gran ordered before she died. It's still in the box in the garage. Maybe we should put it together?" He grinned, warming her from the inside. "That sounds like a good plan. That's what we'll do today then. Plus, we should check your supplies, see what we need, and stock up. Gas for the stoves and whatnot, check the water supply, petrol for the cars, dry goods."

She nodded. Everything he said was sensible.

"How well do you know your neighbors?" He spoke slowly, and she felt a bubble of panic in her chest because their well-being hadn't even occurred to her before.

"Most of them I know fairly well. It's an established, stable neighborhood. Your house was empty after the Friars moved away. And the only other newer family are the Chandras. They moved in about three years ago, and Mrs. Chandra got involved in the local neighborhood center. Thought she knew better, got elected to the board, and turned it upside down so that every dispute in the area became this big mountain, and then she couldn't cope with the stress. She's a nightmare." Elaine shuddered just thinking about the woman who caused all manner of issues for the entire area.

"I saw there's a DIY store around the corner. Plus, I'm sure I heard some hens." "That would be Mrs. Garmin's place."

"We should check on your neighbors, and I noticed most of you have high fences. It might be worth doing something more substantial around the block. There's only what, ten maybe twelve houses?"

"Nine actually. We have a small park at the back of most of the houses."

"Good. That means it can be planted if necessary. What about a water source?"

She nodded at his words. "I get you. We have a small bore on it, as the council uses it to green the area, it's powered by solar panels. Most of the houses also have solar panels, which means basic connectivity is fine while there's good weather. But in winter..." Elaine shrugged.

"What kind of jobs does everyone around here have?"

"Uh, Mr. Garmin was an electrician and Mrs. Frederick's son, who lives nearby, is a plumber."

When Liam smiled her heart fluttered. "Even better. If we've got people around who can help us to hunker down and get through this... Make a list of everyone in the area, their job and skills. We'll load up in an hour or so and get out and around. Check on everyone."

For the first time since this had happened Elaine felt confident they could weather what lay ahead.

*** *

Liam didn't want to frighten Elaine, but he felt sure that they were in this for the long haul. As in years. Now was the time to make arrangements, to lay in supplies, and to form a community that could ride the situation out. That meant they'd have to find animals for food, grow plants that were edible, and secure a water source. It meant taking chances and doing anything necessary to protect what was theirs.

They'd need able bodies to raise the fences higher and make them more substantial. They'd need animals for food and gardens, people who had green fingers. It wouldn't hurt to have some weaponry on hand too. Empty houses could be set up for young families...

In his mind, the list grew. He wasn't a list maker, but judging by the list he saw on the fridge and the one in the small office area, Elaine was. They'd need someone to keep their information up to date, and she was just the girl for that.

His phone buzzed on his hip, and glancing down, he checked the caller ID. "Ramon?"

"Yeah. This is bigger than anyone planned for. We've lost three staff overnight, and the place is in chaos. Can you swing by and get me? It's not real safe here, and the staff are being sent home."

"No worries, I'll get Elaine and we'll be on our way in a couple of minutes."

Elaine's steps told him she was heading downstairs, and a plan was forming in his mind. "Elaine, I need to go get Ramon. Can you take me?"

She smiled. "Of course. Let me get my purse and keys."

While she did that, he pushed heavier furniture in front of the door. That was a priority they would deal with later today.

The drive to the hospital was quick, and he relayed that Ramon would be waiting in the locked vestibule outside. When they pulled up, there he was, standing by the large doors, watching through the plates of glass. He piled in and they headed to Elaine's house. Once they'd settled, Liam asked Elaine to make coffee while Ramon went next door to shower and change. When he returned, Liam waited for them to sit at the table.

"I have got a plan. I was thinking over what you told me, Elaine. We've got a nine-house block plus the park. We can defend ourselves with a little extra work on defenses. We have a doctor in Ramon, plumber, electrician. Some garden basics and even chickens. We need to get the neighbors onside and form a community. We saw what happened last night when that guy tried to break in. There's safety in numbers."

Ramon looked at him stunned. "You want to form an enclave?"

"No, brother, I want to ensure these people in the local area are safe and self-sufficient. We've got shamblers—"

"Zombies actually. They're dead, just reanimated. There is no brain pattern as such..." Liam stared at his brother. "What?"

"Well, the doctors who were still there had been seeing this since the outbreak last week.

All brain activity ceases and the body is simply on an automatic pilot if you will. I had a chance to look at one last night. He died in the ER, and I saw his readings. Quite interesting that the body is able to continue after brain death. Anyway, they—"

"Hang on, what caused the death?"

"Oh, he had come in looking sick. Had taken on a greenish pallor, increased respiration and heart rate, high temps. It looked like a poison, but before he died he told us he'd been bitten by a zombie. I'd say they're on the money with the idea that it's spread by saliva or body fluids. Most of those scratched are contaminated by the blood on their attacker's hands."

"How long from infection to death?" Liam needed to know as much as possible. "Twelve to twenty-four hours seems to be the range. Depends on the person."

"It can spread really fast?"

"Yeah. I've not yet heard of anyone who was infected that didn't succumb."

Elaine sat there, silently taking notes, and Liam wondered what was going through her mind. "We need to batten down. I wonder how long the virus will remain active, because don't they have a certain lifespan?" she asked.

He blinked at her words.

Ramon straightened in his chair, glanced at the woman, and smiled as if she'd asked one of those important life-changing questions. "That's an excellent question. Only problem is it's a week old, and from what I've gleaned, it's spread throughout the country already. Even if we go home—"

"We won't outrun it. Okay then, here's my plan..."

CHAPTER 3

*E*laine knocked on every door, and everyone except the Chandras and Gideons answered. Liam stayed beside her, his hand on the pistol she'd spied on his hip, as they made their way into neighbor after neighbor's house and explained the situation, who Liam and Ramon were, and gave a brief overview of what they hoped to accomplish. Mrs. Garmin broke out in tears, while Mr. Fairweather hugged her hard enough to almost break her ribs.

At the two houses where no one answered, Ramon went around the back, checked inside, and called for Liam's assistance while she was secured in the vehicle. She didn't ask what they were doing, but after the two visits his face was grim and his clothes grubbier than before.

All the neighbors agreed to meet in her backyard at two in the afternoon where Liam would share his plan. It felt like a great plan, except for the part where they'd have to break into the garden center, the hardware store, and the grocery store again. But on the other hand, they needed to prepare for the long haul.

The sun beat down as Elaine carried trays of glasses and mugs. The urn her grandmother had kept for gardening parties and gatherings was full and steaming. Cold lemonade sat in jugs on the small, outdoor table, and she'd even managed to find a couple of packets of biscuits.

"Uh, welcome everyone. You've all met Liam, and this is his brother Ramon, who's an epidemiologist. They've got news and a plan for our safety. Liam is a police officer from the north who has a lot of experience dealing with riots and the like, so I guess that means he's in a good position to help us plan."

She moved to the seat she'd tagged for herself and sat down to watch the two brothers in action.

They'd agreed Liam should go first with the information they'd gleaned. "As you know, the situation right now is pretty bad. We've got a virus that's a week old. Ramon can talk about that in more detail in a moment, but it's decimating the country, leaving us the shamblers who bite and scratch. I've been talking with those who know as well as making contact with the various news stations. Things are bad. People are being urged to form communities, safe places to shelter where there is food and some form of security. We're in a perfect situation here—"

"You want us to feed and shelter others?" a voice from the crowd called out, and Elaine

Love at the End of the World 184

was sure it was old Mrs. Murdock. She'd been crotchety forever, and it seemed an epidemic wasn't improving her attitude.

"No. What I am saying though is there are nine houses and two are effectively empty."

No one commented at Liam's bald statement. They didn't need to, because she could see the way shoulders slumped and faces blanked.

"We have a lot of fencing already in place, and with some effort and equipment from the hardware store, we can reinforce our situation. We already have a range of skills and abilities. We have an electrician, and Mrs. Frederick's son is a plumber, and I'm sure he'd join us. We have a doctor, and no doubt there are some gardeners too."

Gerald Forter raised his hand. "I was in the military as was Mickey Evans here. We served together in East Timor."

She grinned. They were already thinking like a community.

"My suggestion is we pool resources. Turn backyards into vegetable patches. Collect the chickens and find a rooster or two. Breed our own hens. We've got solar on the roof and know- how. We can ride this out. Stay safe."

"We wouldn't have to deal with shamblers? James could keep his family safe?" Mrs. Frederick's voice trembled.

Elaine stood up. "James can bring his family with him, move into one of the empty houses, and raise his kids here. And we can protect ourselves from the shamblers. We all work together with the gardening and keeping the water source clear. We can survive right here in our own homes. We can welcome a couple of other families too. When things improve, we can loosen up what we have. The sheds would be ideal for long-term food storage, and with our own doctor in Ramon, we can be comfortable. We just need to work together."

"I don't agree. I just want to go to my sister's in Queensland. She said there's no sickness there. My daughter is coming tomorrow." Mrs. Murdock scrambled to her feet. "You can leave me out of your planning."

"But Mrs. Murdock, we can't enclose the area without—"

The older woman clomped off as Elaine watched, mystified by her behavior. She shadowed her to the gate and caught sight of a number of bandages applied to Mrs. Murdock's neck. "Mrs. Murdock, what happened?"

The woman turned, and Elaine noted the greenish tinge in her skin. She thought over

Love at the End of the World 185

Ramon's words. Temperature, increased respiration and heart rate. As Elaine stared at her, she noticed the woman was breathing more rapidly than normal.

"Were you bitten or scratched?" Elaine's voice sounded husky.

The older woman simply sniffed at her, then turned and continued through the gate, slamming it after her.

Elaine fastened the latch and returned to the others who were listening to Ramon. "Mrs. Murdock was either scratched or bitten."

A chorus of sympathy filled the air and washed over Elaine who wanted to cry.

Liam crouched beside her. "I'm sorry, Elaine. Truly sorry this is how things are happening."

She sighed. "I know."

The meeting continued, and the rest of the neighbors agreed to the plan. Mr. Forter offered his utility and trailer while Mrs. Garmin said she had a friend with two roosters. She and her birds hadn't been able to find a new home in the suburbs before the outbreak but would be welcomed into their new community. "We can set up a second pen and some brooding areas. Eggs and food to eat."

Elaine tugged out the list of jobs she'd thought could be allocated, and by four o'clock it was planned that the next day they'd start with the garden center, finding seedlings, pots, soil, and seeds to begin their plantings. The men even promised to look out for a couple of greenhouses. She would work with the ladies and draw up a list of what was urgent for the garden, and once the men had those in hand, they'd begin looking at tinned and dry goods, storage options, and start dividing everything up while the men worked on the fencing.

Within a couple of days, they'd be set. If everything went to plan.

*** *

The garden center was quiet, and Liam thought that was fairly unnerving. Forter and Mickey Evans had joined himself, Ramon, and Elaine, dragging carts, ready to fill. Her list seemed fairly extensive, and the scent of fertilizers and chemicals tickled his nose.

"We need corn, lettuce, cucumber, tomato, and herbs, among others. Mrs. Garmin also said we need bee-attracting flowers. I'm not much of a gardener, but let's see about some rosemary, lavender, and stuff like that. Also, if we can find some chamomile? I like tea when I'm stressed, and I think I'm going to be a fair bit of that." She led the charge, heading to the seedlings and crowing when she found what she wanted. Whole trays of everything went into her cart, then she trotted off to some larger trees and started grabbing them.

"What are you doing?" He watched as she picked up four identical trees, then grabbed four more of a different variety.

"We'll need fruit too. Mr. Evans, could you grab me a few dozen large pots, then we can move them into the greenhouse as necessary."

Watching Elaine in action was like following a general, she called out requests and the men scurried to fulfill her desires. She found a roll of shade cloth and ordered it into the trailer along with three greenhouses, a pergola, two barbeques, and a dozen gas bottles.

She scooped up seeds by the handful and added tools, oils, and pesticides. "We don't know when we'll get another chance. So, if we're going to need it, best to grab it now."

Finally satisfied, they secured their load and climbed into the vehicle. It was eerie on the quiet roads, and the lack of people kept Liam on his guard. At the house, he told them to deposit everything in the backyard.

She climbed out. "I'll get the women, and we'll hit the grocery store."

He frowned. "Wait for back up."

Mickey Evans followed Elaine and sighed as if he'd realized the women were ready to get to work now. "I'll go with them. As long as we stay together and move quickly, it should be all right."

Liam wasn't comfortable with that but agreed. The sooner they had what they needed, the sooner they could hunker down again. "Take a car. Back up to the shop."

"I'll go one better, Liam. We're taking three. Mine, Emily's, and Mrs. Garmin's SUV, and depending on how much we collect, we can make several trips. We'll be in and out before anyone notices."

Liam frowned, worrying about the women, as he and the others drove off, heading to the hardware store. The fencing was easy to find and they loaded quickly. He also suggested more tools, hammers, nails and screws, quickset concrete, and a jackhammer among other items. The men looked at him as if he were mad, but they hurried to collect everything, and by the time they'd pulled into the B-and-B's yard he was exhausted.

"Ramon, can you go see if—"

Shouts and bangs echoed. A shot cracked in the air, and he was out of his seat, running.

Because they'd returned via the back end of the property, they hadn't seen the crowd gathering at the store across the road. Twenty or more zombies and the women, screaming. He shot forward, legs pumping as fury and fear coalesced inside him. Elaine. Where is Elaine?

CHAPTER 4

The zombies had come up on them quickly, taking the small group by surprise as they loaded slow cookers, two bread machines, what felt like a ton of ten-kilo bags of bread mix, and slabs of flour into the vehicle. Mr. Evans had blocked the way with the SUV, but the shambling zombies were determined, arms swinging, teeth bared, nails sharp and ready to rake unsuspecting humans. And there was Emily in the middle of the throng, eyes blank, skin rotting while the stench threatened to overcome Elaine.

Mr. Evans fired again and another zombie went down. The women behind Elaine cowered. She heard yells as the zombies turned like a slow sea. Clambering onto the back of her sedan, she noted with horror that Liam and Ramon were there, joined by Mr. Forter, his double- barreled shotgun primed and pointed.

Elaine watched as Liam focused, face and eyes flat. His expression was hard, betraying no inner turmoil as his finger squeezed the trigger. He shot one dead center in the forehead, and it dropped and stayed down, unlike the one Mickey Evans had hit in the leg. It pulled itself toward them, fingers scrabbling on the concrete, seeking purchase. It reached out toward Mrs. Garmin, its eyes shining with a hungry gleam.

"Mrs. Garmin!" Elaine yanked the older woman back.

Without conscious thought, Elaine swung the tire iron in her hand and hit the zombie in the head, smashing with a crunch that turned her stomach. It moaned a single, long dirge, and she smashed it again. The sound stopped as did the actions, and she stared at what she'd done then glanced at Mrs. Garmin, whose shocked gaze had settled on Elaine.

She looked back to the men who were clearing the last few zombies, Emily nowhere to be seen, and sighed. "We should get the rest of the stuff on our list."

It felt odd to be standing there, surrounded by bits of what was once a person, and demanding that they finish their shopping, but if they were to survive, this was the only way.

Her own trolley stood empty, and she grabbed it and turned back to find coffee, tea, sugar, sweeteners, and other items on her list. No one spoke now; the happy chatter that had surrounded her had dissipated. With a single-minded attitude, Elaine scooped up all the underwear, toilet paper, and masses of toiletries. Pharmaceuticals and pain relievers were tipped in by the box along with packs of batteries. They might not get another chance like this, and she'd take every opportunity.

Every plastic container, bin, and cleaning equipment went into their vehicles. As one filled they shuffled the vehicles around, drove back to the houses, unloaded, then returned. There may be other survivors, but their main task was to prepare their community for a long war against whatever had started this.

Finally satisfied they'd fulfilled their wishlists, she clambered into the back of the SUV, then they made their way back to the houses.

Silently, Elaine trudged inside, surprised to find a heavy metal door had been erected at her house and Liam waiting with a steaming coffee on the kitchen bench for her.

"Want to talk?" He grabbed her close and gave her a bone-crushing hug that in her mind spoke volumes before releasing her.

"No," she said. He probably thought she was rude, but that wasn't it.

"What's in that?" he asked, gesturing to the rucksack that hung low in her hand.

She tugged the bag closer, feeling foolish. "Nothing. I'm going to shower."

Up the stairs she went, two at a time. If he'd seen what she'd grabbed, she'd just die. She stashed the bag loaded with condoms, lubricant, and even pregnancy tests in her wardrobe and stripped off, stepping into the shower stall. As she washed she considered the items in the bag. Who knew if and when they'd be needed, but it had seemed sensible when she'd scooped them up. Now she just felt foolish.

When she returned downstairs, Ramon was looking through the piles of antihistamines, codeine, and cough medicines she'd snatched. She noted Liam wasn't around. "Where's Liam?"

"He was needed in the garden to move something."

"Oh." There didn't seem to be anything else for her to add, so she looked at Ramon, hoping for some kind of direction on what to do next.

"You did good. We should hit a pharmacy next. Grab some basic drugs, antibiotics, etcetera. Mrs. Garmin has a guest suite at her place, and she's going to let me set it up as a surgery. She used to be a nurse, so that's an assist, and there's a big fridge freezer for the drugs and things. We can reinforce it easily with the metal bars and security screening, and it's in the back area, so not able to be seen from the front."

Elaine nodded.

"Look, I know I haven't been exactly nice to you," Ramon said. "Liam is all I have, and until now, I planned to go home, but there's no benefit in it. I found Mrs. Murdock, or what's left of the woman she'd been. She's turned into a zombie, and Mickey and Mr. Forter are out there now dealing with her. I couldn't. The same way I couldn't have done what you did today at the store. But you saved lives. You reacted to protect. You're stronger than me like that. We need to pull together and respect each other. And you earned that today."

She wasn't sure she quite liked the fact that she had to earn his respect, but the way she felt about his brother meant that if she wanted to form a relationship with Liam—and that seemed increasingly likely if the hug he'd given her on her return from the shop was an indicator—then they had to find a way to agree and work together.

"Great. Do you know when the men are planning to start putting up the fencing?" she asked.

He smiled at her, moved to the curtains, and pulled them aside. The men worked side by side digging holes and laying out the concrete mix.

She watched them work for a moment or two. "Quick workers."

"Sure are. And Mrs. Frederick's son and daughter-in-law and their two kids arrived earlier. Her sister and husband and their three are due soon as well. Carrie—Mrs. Frederick's daughter-in-law—is a teacher and Sarna, her sister, is a police officer. Jeff, the husband, is a builder. We've got a great little community going on here. With Mr. Forter and Mickey Evans, we should be okay for security. What we are missing though is some basic medical equipment. A heart monitor, pressure cuffs, etcetera. I can't go grab them from the hospital because others will need them."

Now Elaine smiled. "I know where you can get that from. I'm guessing you'll also need sterile procedure packs, oxygen and masks. Cleansers and—"

He looked at her stunned. "Where?"

"The place I used to work. We could go there tomorrow. I need to help the women set up the storage of dry goods first."

He rubbed his hands together, and she couldn't help but grin.

"There's also some basic lab-work equipment. Make a list of what you want. It'll make it easier." With that said, she retreated to where the others waited, outside in the backyard amid mountains of boxes. "Right, let's clear out the garages, lay down the rodent repellant, and get to work."

It was a long, hot day, but by the time the sun dipped down she was pleased with what they'd achieved. Every garage had been stocked and catalogued so it would be easy to find what was needed.

The two older women had created a cooking list and a roster for everyone, to make their provisions go further.

The barbeques were set up in the B-and-B's yard while they watered the seedlings that had looked droopy and unloved when delivered. The tables they'd dragged into the garden were set up. The children, subdued by the changes, settled into the middle as the meats they'd found in the storage freezers cooked, scenting the air.

"We need to get rid of the bodies." Ramon spoke quietly.

Liam nodded. "Already on it, brother. Jeff has a bobcat. Brought it with him on a trailer. He's already had it out, dug out a burial pit, and we've collected as many bodies as we could find and covered them."

It was incongruous to be sitting down to a meal while discussing disposing of human remains. But things were changing and their attitudes had to as well. Otherwise they'd pay the price. Sicken and die.

Elaine fiddled with her plate. "We also need to talk about how to cope with others who join us. We have you and your brother in the house next door, but I did wonder if maybe Ramon shouldn't talk to Mrs. Garmin about moving into her house, since they'll be working together. Then we just need to find somewhere for you."

His eyes glinted, and his smile warmed her all over. "I already have that in hand."

"Oh?"

His hand grabbed hers under the table, and a fluttery sensation started in her belly and spread, heated and drugging.

"Here. I plan to stay here in your home. With you."

For a moment she blinked, trying to deal with the confused array of feelings. In some ways it was too soon, yet it also felt right that he was here, sharing her house.

"I, uh..." She bit her lip. "You haven't asked," she said, her voice echoing thick to her hearing.

"May I? Stay here, I mean."

Love at the End of the World 191

"Yes, there's a spare room. I mean..." It was all she could think of for the moment.

Dinner seemed to take forever as she watched those assembled chatter, settle, and become a family. They had to be, she realized, if they were going to get through this.

She met Sarna and Jeff, Carrie and James, and the five children—Tracey, Mark, Charlotte, Elizabeth, and Nicola. They ranged in ages from five to eleven and would no doubt lighten the atmosphere considerably, but it would also place greater strain because they would need the highest level of protection. After all, they were the future of the human race.

Liam cleared his throat. "Carrie said the rumpus room in the house they've moved into will make a good classroom, so that's one less concern. She's also suggested that they have a half-day of academic work and a half-day of on-the-job training. They can learn all the trades from horticulture and building, to washing, cooking, and administration."

Elaine sat back and laughed. "Thinking long term?"

"Something like that. Now, we're both off the washing up roster, and I'm tired and so are you." He eased her up, bade goodnight to all, and steered her back to the house through the connecting gate.

Once inside he checked the windows they'd reinforced with shutters and led her upstairs.

Silence wrapped itself around her like a cocoon. Welcoming, beckoning, and full of promise. At her bedroom door, he stopped, leaned in, and kissed her gently as her lips gave beneath his touch. His hands burrowed under her light shirt to caress the skin of her back.

"Ask me in, Elaine."

She heard the desire in his voice, felt the twin as she fumbled for the door behind her. "Come with me."

As if it were a switch, the burn of passion exploded, his lips roaming and seeking, finding the sensitive hollow where jaw met neck. A shiver of sensation washed over her. Heat pooled in her belly and between her legs, and her nipples tightened to sensitive points.

Her fingers speared into his hair and latched on as he moved closer. Needing more than a kiss to dampen the rampant hunger. She starved for the touch of skin to skin.

The emptiness clawed, and she tugged at his shirt. Desperate now to see him. To touch the hardness she'd felt the last time he'd held her close.

"Shit!" He pulled away. "I don't have any protection."

His words stopped her, left her reeling for a moment, then she grinned. "Not to worry. I do."

The hot burn that had suffused her earlier hit again as she reached for the backpack. As she unzipped it, boxes of condoms and bottles of lubricant dropped to the bed. At least she'd put the pregnancy test kits in another section.

The thought fled when he cupped her breasts, moving behind her so she could feel his desire jutting at her buttocks. "You know, the first time I met you, in that shop, you were already looking after yourself. An amazingly strong woman, capable and caring. I don't know exactly what this emotion I feel for you is, but it warms me, Elaine. I think about you, want to be sure you're safe. I've got no intention of ignoring it. I rely on my instincts too often." Then he kissed her jaw and she sighed her pleasure.

Turning in his arms seemed so natural. Reaching for his shirt, she tugged it over his head so she could feast her eyes on the perfectly sculpted torso. His nipples, pale, flat discs unobscured by hair, had her quaking with a tide of desire. She had a thing for men with bare chests.

Elaine felt the ripple in her nerves as his fingers shook, flicking one then another of her buttons through the holes. "Don't want to rip this shirt." The rasp of his words betrayed him further, and she laughed, tiny and throaty, and for an instant she wondered is this really me?

When Liam bent down and kissed her collarbone, a whisper of lips, she shook, knees like jelly, and she reached out to steady herself, hands settling on his hips. The graze of fingers on bare flesh spurred her on and she slid her fingers down, past the waistband of his jeans, and he hissed.

"You know, I think I need more." Her whisper echoed, and he tugged away.

"Really? Then your wish is my command, madam." His hands settled on the buckle of his belt, his eyes holding hers captive.

Her mouth dried and the insistent hammer of her heart sped up.

"Let... Let me." She brushed his hands aside, even though her own shook madly. She'd only had one other encounter, brief and fumbled in the dark. She'd thought it was everything until now. Now she wanted it all. To see. To experience.

Elaine's fingers fumbled on the end of the belt, tugged, and the prong released. The belt sagged and she found the snap of his pants. It took all her concentration to pop it, her fingers unsteady.

When she reached for the zipper he stopped her. "I don't want to wait, but if I don't, I won't last."

She giggled, womanly power urging her fingers to move as his mouth settled on hers and feasted. The rasp of his zipper sounded. Then his arms were back, winding around her, and suddenly she felt the sag of her breasts as her bra came undone.

With soft hands, he slid the straps down until she was bared at the top, nipples brushing against his chest, and the sensations arced, like electrifying zings.

His mouth moved down the center of her throat and across her collarbone as he touched and caressed and kneaded, and she followed him. Sliding her hands down his back until she felt his buttocks. Hard, firm, and rounded.

Her fingers settled on the flesh, and he whispered against her skin.

Liam grabbed her pants and knickers and pushed them down her legs so she was as naked as he. The air teased her sensitive skin and she hissed, feeling the jerk of his cock against her belly.

Taking her hand, Liam led her to the bed. He brushed off the boxes except for one, and with his gaze firmly on her, he opened it, pulled out a foil pack, and broke it open.

"Put it on me?"

Her tongue felt like it was glued to the top of her mouth. "I... I've never—"

His grin widened. "I'll teach you." He placed the rubber on the head. "Roll it down, sweetheart. All the way."

Nerves jangled between her legs, and she followed his whispered instructions, rolling her hand down his length until it reached his lightly haired sacs. Liam arched up.

"I didn't hurt you, did I?" God knew she'd tried to be gentle.

He groaned. "No, but I want you so badly now, I almost exploded."

She giggled as he pushed her back, one hand sliding between her legs. She stilled, her body aflame for him as he touched her clit. His finger toyed, gliding in the sudden moisture before sliding inside her body.

God, she was so wet. It was embarrassing, yet he seemed happy, eager even as he sighed and touched. "Ready for me."

Elaine's legs shook as he parted them further, settled her legs over his, and leaned in. He kissed her as he slid deeply within, and she sighed with pleasure.

He filled her to the hilt, then stayed still as if he knew she needed slow. Needed the emotion as much as the connection.

The first move was a nudge as his hands found her breasts again, and ever so gently, he rubbed a thumb over one engorged nub. Her clit was tickled by the jutting edge of his shaft, and she shifted, sensations she'd never before known feeding the growing frenzy in her mind.

The second thrust was harder, more insistent, and her hips moved in time, as if a rhythm only they knew determined her actions. It sucked her deeper into the well of sensuality.

From there every action grew wilder and faster. He pulled his lips from hers and inhaled deeply as the scent of lovemaking filled the air around them, heady with musk.

"I'm going to make you come, then again, Elaine. Because this and us? This is heaven."

The urgency increased with every slam home winding the pressure up. Her skin was on fire, and her fingers settled on his shoulders, holding on, needing him closer. Her legs wound around his hips, and she gave him everything. The rub of her breasts against his chest heightened her arousal, and she sobbed, "Please, Liam, more!"

Her body pounded as her heartrate spiked, the hunger growing until it exploded around her, inside her. Spinning her into some kind of bubble where nothing except them and erotic pleasure existed.

She felt him stiffen, heard him call out, then he shuddered in her arms.

Her body turned soft, exhaustion filling every muscle.

Liam collapsed on her. "Holy mother of God." His words were little more than an awed whisper.

"Does that mean..." She swallowed, but her mouth was dry. "Does that mean good?" His bark of laughter was followed swiftly by, "Better than damned good. Awesome." "Good." She closed her eyes and smiled.

CHAPTER 5

*L*iam had never been a morning person, so when day break woke him, he groused and turned over. Something warm was beside him. His eyes opened.

Elaine.

Last night.

Warmth flooded his system. Last night had been so damned good. So very damned good.

He'd never experienced lovemaking of that kind before.

He rolled back, flinging his arms over his eyes. He was in over his head, he knew it and yet... unlike previous relationships and the one that had nearly turned serious, he didn't feel that odd sense of panic.

What does that mean? His emotions were certainly tangled. He didn't want to make a mistake and not take into account the fact that they were in the middle of a zombie apocalypse, but he also didn't see how what he felt could be reliant on human nature demanding he procreate either.

Confusion wasn't a normal state of mind for him, so rather than think and mull, he got up, pulled on his jeans, and headed downstairs to make coffee. In the kitchen he drew up short when he saw Ramon filling the kettle.

"I wasn't going to come upstairs in case you were..."

"I'll have a coffee and Elaine a cup of tea."

Ramon gave him the 'what gives' look, but Liam just shrugged, for the first time unwilling to share anything about the night before. This was special. Between him and Elaine. "Got the consulting room set up yet?"

He'd come downstairs to make tea for Elaine so they could begin the day. With his uncustomary chattiness first thing in the morning, he'd just betrayed his state of mind to his brother.

"Serious, huh?" Ramon said.

He shrugged again, and Ramon shoved a cup of coffee at him and turned back to make Elaine's tea.

"Normally you'd tell me she's amazing or wonderful. The fact you're keeping your mouth shut about the woman tells me you're over your heels for her. She's well thought of. The others were concerned, and Evans and Forter were heading over to check on her when we arrived at their doors. They're worried you're going to take advantage of her." Ramon pierced him with a look. "So, we're staying then?"

The thought of leaving tore him up inside. "Yeah, I'm staying. There's nothing for us in Queensland anymore, unless you have a woman stashed away. They need me here, and you too."

Ramon shrugged. "Women are in short supply right now, so I'll wait and see what happens next. By the way, apparently there's a school two blocks over. By my reckoning there's enough land there to cultivate and run some stock. Evans has a brother who raises cows and sheep. He said if we could make a paddock or two safe for livestock, we could bring the brother and his extended family of nine kids, eight adults, and a good-sized herd in. They could provide meat and milk. A couple of their neighbors also arrived last night at the brother's house. They have horses and a dozen pigs, plus more hens and roosters. We could be almost self-sufficient."

"How did you find all this out?"

"After you left, Evans' cellphone rang. The others agree with the plan. They'll be here tomorrow, so some of the men are heading over there to change the locks, fortify, and get ready. There are spare beds in the houses here, and our friends are planning the layout. We need to be quick though, collecting the medications and so on, because Mrs. Garmin and I think we could take over three of the classrooms. One for a ward, a nursery as we have two pregnant women on the way, an operating theatre and a dispensary slash consulting room."

"So, did Elaine get formula, nappies, and the like?"

"No, I didn't. But we can go back. Grab those things and toddler items, because we'll need them," Elaine replied as she walked into the kitchen. Liam turned and scooped up the tea to hand to her. "We can do that after we get the medical supplies. It also wouldn't hurt to find furniture. We can scout out some of the houses nearby and see what we can find."

The smile she turned on him was full of emotion and he felt six-foot-tall and all male.

"There's a furniture store nearby if that would be better, they've got a babies and children's section. If we could find a truck or something, we could set them up with everything they need. Linen too. We could also do with a couple of washing machines, because with babies, we'll need to launder diapers." Elaine sipped her drink.

Ramon nodded. "Might be better to go with new, particularly because we don't know what viruses we'll find in any blood or body fluids."

"Fine, and more kitchen gear too. It was a primary school, and while there'll be fridges,

I'm not totally sure what they have in the canteen in the way of cooking equipment." She turned to Ramon. "Give me twenty minutes and I'll be ready to go. We'll need the utility and trailer for everything you need, and I'm guessing you have the list ready?"

He handed it over and Liam scanned the sheet of paper with a typed list. "Good thing you printed it, your handwriting is atrocious."

"They teach us that in med school so no one can copy it." With a smirk, Ramon headed for the door. "We'll meet in twenty minutes out front."

*** *

They made quick work of the drive, but Elaine's knees knocked the whole way. What if Mr. Eckerman was still there? She'd grabbed the keys to the office and facility and stashed them in the pocket of her jeans. They drove in the borrowed SUV into the back and she used the small remote device to lift the security gate so they could drive in.

Only after the gates shut did they open the car doors. "If Mr. Eckerman is here, he'll be in the office. I'll go in an—"

"Not alone, you won't." Liam grabbed her hand. "All it takes is a bite or scratch, Elaine. I'm not going to risk you." He brushed a stray strand of hair from her face, cupped it gently, and smiled. "We go in together."

"Okay." She made it to the steps before she heard the sound.

Liam moved in front of her, his hand on his hip, digging out the tiny pistol. "Stay behind me."

His hand was on the door before she could stop him, so she gripped it. "We can look through this window here. See if he's in there." Elaine pulled him along the balcony so they could glance in, then wished she hadn't. "Oh no!"

Three zombies were inside, feeding.

Her gut churned, because what she saw was Eckerman, or the remains of him.

"He must have tried to go out the front. I told him not to. He insisted we should stay

here." Regret colored her words. "He never liked parking in the back because he'd had the business name stenciled on his car." She didn't dare breathe too deeply because of the stench emanating from the shamblers, but she firmed her will. "Come on, we should head downstairs to the facility and load up."

Elaine refused to look back but said a prayer for the soul of Mr. Eckerman, then set to the task of loading the items Ramon had requested into the vehicle and trailer. They wouldn't have everything, but they'd come close.

It was hard work, lifting and sorting. After two hours they'd loaded the autoclave, the sterile surgical kits, heart monitor, humid-crib, lab equipment, and oxygen. They also found and added a couple of IV drip stands and some additional items he'd seen and just had to have.

"Well, that's almost everything on Ramon's list. We should head past a pharmacy on our way back so we can load up." Elaine folded the list then shoved it into the molded pocket of the car door.

Ramon grunted his approval, and they tied everything down after covering their stash with the cloths they'd brought with them.

Once back on the road, she drove to the nearest pharmacy. Liam sat beside her, his pistol resting on his lap. She was dismayed to see the window of the pharmacy had been kicked in. As before, Liam moved in front of her then stood sentinel as they loaded up a couple of wheelchairs, every formula tin they could find, nappies, various analgesics and bandages, dressings and sterilization gear, baby goods, and lastly medications from behind the counter.

"Good thing you grabbed those cold boxes to throw in with ice bricks, otherwise we'd be compromising everything. Good work too on the vaccines and hypos." Ramon quickly moved the box into the boot, wedging them firmly as they glanced outside.

Liam muttered something unintelligible. Even though the roads were still quiet, something felt even more distinctly off than before. Then he growled, "We need to get out of here."

She ushered them to the door as she saw a small army of shufflers. "Oh my God. We have to get out of here, now!"

They jumped into the vehicle, packets shoved to the back seat and into Ramon's waiting arms while Liam aimed on the small but advancing crowd.

Elaine gunned the engine and sped off down the road. There were more at every turn, and the liquid in her stomach felt like it had turned to concrete, the weight of it almost too much to bear.

She drove as fast as she could into the school grounds then parked by the building they'd earmarked. Elaine was about to hit the horn when Liam shook his head. "No. We don't want to announce ourselves to the zombies. We need to be quick, unload then head off to the next job." Thankfully, the armies of undead hadn't yet descended on this area, so they moved with speed, unloading and securing the items upstairs where Ramon reasoned they'd be best protected. "They seem to go for the weakest first, like it's some kind of sense, so we need the sick, injured, and youngest as far away from them as possible."

At least they'd had help unloading. The new residents had arrived with trucks, motorhomes, and caravans, their number swelling by nearly forty adults and thirteen children, and they all pitched in.

"Get the kids upstairs and secure the animals in the buildings that have been cleared," Liam instructed. "There are zombies headed this way and we haven't yet increased the security on this site." Liam gave them his cell number, then they headed back to the community.

Only when they were settled back in her house did the hideous pounding of Elaine's heart slow down.

"I'm almost out of petrol for the car, Liam. We're going to have to secure a supply if we continue like this. And with more animals we'll need to find feed and store it in a secure location."

It seemed to her that as fast as they solved problems more cropped up, and that included the added issue of housing all the newcomers.

"Yeah, I know. I don't have an easy answer for that."

She could see the worry settling on his shoulders, so she reached over and rubbed them, hoping to alleviate the tension she sensed. It all seemed so natural to her, dealing with Liam. He wasn't like Davey, her one and only boyfriend, who'd found her confusing, as he'd put it.

CHAPTER 6

The meal that night was more subdued as the adults sat in one yard and the children played in another.

Liam addressed the assembled crowd. "We need more supplies. We need animal fodder, more fencing supplies, ammunition, and gas. Also, furniture. It feels like we're constantly chasing our tails and—"

"Boy, you three have taken on a lot already. Some of us can do more." Mrs. Garmin nodded as she spoke. "We've been chatting today. Jeff and Stuart can round up men to start the fencing on the main area of the school. They can also arrange for the trucks that brought the animals in to collect the fencing needed. Hell, they can even add in a walkway between the community and the school, safe enough for everyone to come and go. Most of the women are able to lift and carry and can help with collecting furniture and clothing, which we'll be needing more of. And we'll find other jobs for the ones who can't. It wouldn't hurt to lay our hands on some material and sewing machines and they may be able to sew or learn. We move on a roster, just like Elaine did for the cooking. We're going to need people to run the show, and it seems to me like you two already have that under control. So delegate and let others go out and do what they can. Us older folk can mind the kids, dig the gardens, and plant. We could even build animal houses."

The men and women nodded and murmured their agreement, and Liam felt overwhelmed. They hadn't known him from a stick a week ago, and now they declared he needed to delegate better. *It's exactly what my sergeant used to tell me.*

"All right then. But you'll need lists."

Elaine was there sliding her hand over his. "I can handle that. I need to know numbers and sizes so we can plan accordingly. Get them to me in the morning and we'll work out a suitable roster. My house is big enough that we can make it the headquarters for now, until we can arrange something better." Then she leaned over and kissed his ear. "We'll be fine, and they're right, we need to have others do parts of the set up. We're no longer the only able ones around."

*E*laine stretched until the banging started on the door downstairs then rolled over and groaned. "Ugh, it's barely any daylight. It's too soon for visitors."

"Maybe, but they took you at your word and are lined up at the front door. Up and at it, Ms. Administrator. I'll get you a tea while you dress."

Liam slid a kiss onto her lips, and for an instant she pondered about not only how right it felt to be with him, but how easily she'd made the transition.

She dragged on jeans and t-shirt, wound her hair up into a loose bun, and brushed her teeth before descending the stairs.

Liam was in the small hallway in jeans with bare feet and a half-buttoned shirt, and he offered her the hot drink.

"I told them to wait until you've had your coffee, otherwise you won't get a chance to stop." Liam's voice rasped, and she shivered, ricochets of last night's sensuality threading through her.

"You didn't ask them to come in?"

He cocked his head to one side and smiled. "It's your home...our home. It's nice outside, and there's coffee and tea for them while they wait."

She snickered and ogled his chest for a moment then sighed. "I'd better get to work." Then she headed for the door to find out what they needed.

The morning passed with list making, and it was well after ten by the time she turned on the television.

"This is the last broadcast of Channel One. The government has collapsed. Overnight the last senior politicians, their families, and staff were airlifted from the national base and moved to an undisclosed location. The police and all emergency services have disbanded. Pockets of armed services are patrolling, but there is now no official law. We have reports of mobs of zombies on the streets, and gangs as well. A gunfight taking place on the lawns of parliament house and rounding up of civilians. We have been advised to seek safety, as far away from heavily populated areas as possible. Arm yourselves, keep your children indoors, and stock up. This broadcast will be replayed on a loop. Alert friends and neighbors to prepare for the worst.

Stay safe, and may God have mercy on our souls. This is Kadey Stainhouse signing off for the very last time." The woman's face faded away, but not before the white visage and the trail of tears hit Elaine like a ton of bricks.

Elaine stood stock-still, shock and horror pounding at her brain. She wanted to yell it's not true, but with everything that was going on, she very much feared this was their new reality. Liam entered the room, and she turned like an automaton.

"What's wrong?" He moved quickly to her side and rubbed her arms with a look of alarm on his face.

"It's all over. The government's gone. Police and emergency services released, and gangs...zombies... What are we going to do?" She heard the rising tide of hysteria in her voice but couldn't seem to control it.

"We do what we've been doing, just faster. I need to get hold of Ramon and the teams out collecting, and tell them to get back here asap. We need that school reinforced now! I'll check out front. Get onto Ramon and his team, Elaine."

With trembling hands, she did as he demanded, contacting Ramon on the cell, then stopped as men armed with rifles entered her tiny living area. "What... What's going on?"

"A gang headed this way. There's got a man on a motorcycle leading them. We suspect he's the one that tried to get in here."

It was too much. She simply stood up and left the room for the kitchen.

*** *

After Liam talked with the assembled men, he joined Elaine in the kitchen. "You okay?"

She turned and the expression on her face surprised him. "I didn't expect this to be easy, not once we realized what was going on. But to be honest, I'll be buggered if someone thinks they can take away from us what we've built already." She dumped coffee into two cups and poured in boiled water.

"They won't. Our community is preparing themselves to protect what we made. They've started the process of patrolling, with Mickey finding a spot in one of the empty houses. He'll ring us as soon as they see something we need to know about."

"All right."

"So, what do you want me to do?" he asked. "Grab me the milk first."

Love at the End of the World 203

He took it out of the fridge and handed it over. "That wasn't what I mean."

"I know." Elaine sighed and measured some into the mugs. "I want to stop the world for a while, push the problems aside, and create a bubble, and I know that's not going to happen. I want to know what's going on with us, but it's new and these things take time. I know that too." She turned and leaned against the cupboards. "Liam, I know there's something special about us, the relationship we're growing, but—"

The phone on his hip buzzed and she stopped, inhaling deeply as he answered.

"They're on their way. Three vehicles and a motorbike. I can see a couple of rifles. There's seven people I can see. They're turning the corner now." Mickey Evans gave his brief report.

He pierced her with his gaze. "We'll finish this later."

Elaine simply nodded. There wasn't anything else to say.

"Thanks, Mickey. Head on over, remember to come up the back and use the automatic door."

"Will do."

Liam turned to Elaine. "Would you consider staying in here?"

"No." Elaine answered as he expected, though he'd hoped she'd answer differently.

"All right then. Follow me."

She shadowed him to the door where he waited, hand on the butt of his pistol, behind the

barrier of their quickly thrown up eight-foot-high fencing.

The vehicles came to a sharp stop next to the motorcycle, and the thug who'd tried to

break in clambered off the bike. "I want the woman," the man bellowed, and Liam opened the security door to step outside, glad they'd made such speed erecting chain link fence around the community.

He nearly hissed when he heard Elaine. "I make my own decisions, and you aren't what I want."

The man bared his teeth and raised his rifle. "Don't much care, girl."

Liam smiled as the windows of the house opened upstairs and down, along with the ones next door.

The metal barrels of the rifles his men pointed out at the intruders stayed still, trained on the vehicles. Liam took a step closer to the fence. "You don't get a say, friend. Walk or drive away now and we won't take offense. Push off or face the consequences."

"Screw you." Motorcycle Man spat on the asphalt.

Above Liam, the click of an engaged barrel sounded, and then there was a boom, and asphalt flew beside Motorcycle Man's feet.

Liam grinned. "That's your warning. Leave. Now." He raised his pistol.

The man wavered. Liam pulled back on the hammer of his pistol, and the man climbed onto the motorbike. "I'll be back, and I'll take what I want."

He wasn't fast enough though as Jeff screamed a warning from the house next door.

"Shufflers incoming. At least thirty. Lock down the community!"

The man laughed. "You're full of shit!"

Motorcycle Man revved the engine. Elaine gulped loudly as if the massacre that was pending was already running through her mind like a video. Liam had no intention of watching on as they attacked. He'd order everyone to head inside in a moment, he just needed to make the point that they were on their home ground.

"Liam?" she said.

"They're still alive. They can get away if they leave now." Liam felt her hand burrow into his grip as they waited, the man watching them, his face turning beet red as he noted their connection.

The sound grew, the moan and shuffle of numerous feet.

"I can't stay." Elaine released his fingers and headed inside. Before he followed her, he turned. "We could save you, if you promise to leave as soon as it's safe and not return."

The man scoffed. "I don't think so. I take what I want, and I want her and this." Motorcycle Man waved his hands, and Liam simply shrugged and headed into the house.

"Shut the doors and windows. Close the shutters and curtains. Keep the children in the back, away from what's happening, and alert the school," Liam demanded.

People moved, phones to ears relaying his orders. Elaine turned and retreated into the house.

The screech of one car then another told him some had gone, but the revving of the bike continued. Liam trudged into the kitchen, sending Elaine to the backyard and away from the sounds that he knew would echo, hoping the trees would offer a sound buffer.

Then he heard the sound he'd hoped not to hear. The strident scream that told of pain and fear. The stomach-curdling sound stopped, ending abruptly. He grabbed the coffee she'd made him earlier and they'd abandoned, and sipped it even though he felt decidedly ill. He felt no pleasure in what had transpired, only a sense of relief that the man wouldn't come after Elaine again. It answered the question that had rolled around in his mind. Did he love Elaine? Yes, he did. So now he needed to tell her.

He slid out the back door and found her sitting in a chair, tears in her eyes. "He's dead, right?"

"I think so, Elaine." When she sniffled, he sighed and settled down beside her. "I want to talk to you."

"You're revolted that I'm a wimp?"

He couldn't help but laugh, but she'd sounded so glum, and he took her hand in his. "No. Actually, you're amazing, and I love you, Elaine." Shock filled her face and he laughed again. "Needing to protect you from that man? That made me face the fact that I was hedging and ignoring the truth. We could easily lose sight of anything positive. But you and what we've built in a really short time, and not just the intimacy—though that's absolutely outstanding and amazing, by the way—it's more about hope. We're building a community and a family, but that's extraneous when it comes to what I feel about you." He grabbed her hand, thudded it against his chest. "Inside me there's this bubble of hope and love, and it's growing because you make me happy. You stand beside me, not behind, and that's what I've wanted all my life. I love you, Elaine, and if we can find a way to make it official, I'll take it with both hands, when you're ready."

Elaine's shock gave way to tears as she launched into his embrace, plastering herself against him. "I can't believe that in all this mess, I met you. I'm not sure just yet that I love you, but I feel this connection." Her balled fist settled against her chest as if she released some bubble of frustration from inside her. He knew she was cautious, but clearly she knew and accepted there was potential for the future growing between them.

Liam would accept that for now and hope for the future.

"There aren't enough words to explain the confusion and everything I feel, Liam. I want this so badly, but I haven't got the experience to know. I'm going to need time but not space, okay? Because I need you, and I don't yet understand that either."

She hiccupped and snuggled in and he took the moment and the opportunity offered.

CHAPTER 7

$\mathcal{E}$laine rubbed her hands over the back of her neck. Summer had set in with a vengeance, and here she was three days before Christmas, trying to ensure the kids had some sense of festivity.

Ten of the young cockerels would be roasted, and she thanked Mrs. Garmin for her foresight in setting up a breeding program. There was a bevy of women taking turns to run the spit they'd fashioned for these kinds of occasions. Fluffy feathers seemed to have adhered themselves to Elaine's clothes and hands from assisting with the plucking.

The salad would be picked fresh on Christmas morning, and while there wouldn't be a huge number of presents, Liam had arranged a surprise for the children—a piñata filled with new items from a store they'd visited several weeks before. There would even be a new book for every child, including a range of board books for the newly-born addition and the nearly-there one who was due any day.

Liam. Now he made her smile day after day. Each night was a wonderland of erotic sensuality, and during the day he took every opportunity to show her just how caring he was—no mean feat as he'd become the leader of the community, democratically elected.

The coffee in her cup had turned cold as she sat looking at it. "So why haven't I told him I love him yet?" Initially she'd had concerns about Ramon, well aware he wasn't as keen on her. But he was thawing and that certainly was a help.

The walkie-talkie beside her sqwarked. "Elaine? Nina's in labor, and we need Ramon at the surgery."

"Okay. He's out back with Liam. I'll get him and send him down."

She placed the device face-down and headed to what had once been her backyard. Now it was a mass of green and red, planted with tomatoes, corn, and lettuce. The two men were weeding, a task shared equally by all members of the community.

"Ramon? Nina's in labor, and they need you."

He indicated with a wave that he'd heard and she moved down the yard as he set off at an amble.

"He looks happy and rested. Really different from what he was like when I first met him."

"He met someone in the latest intake. A girl called Sarah who is a refugee from Sydney. She'd been biking down here when the epidemic took hold and a family kind of adopted her. He's thinking they should take it slow, like us."

Elaine searched Liam's gaze, watching as he brushed the dirt off his hands.

"I think that's looking good." He motioned to the garden. "I never expected to like gardening half this much."

His words stopped her in her tracks. Never expected... "Liam? I've not been fair to you, have I? I mean here you are, working at making a life for all of us, while I've been hiding from the truth."

As she was about to launch into her spiel, Jeff came through the gate. "Liam? When you've got five can I talk to you about an idea for water saving?"

Liam nodded distractedly, his gaze on hers. "Elaine, what do you mean hiding from the truth?" There it was, the tiny chink of uncertainty that she'd avoided and ignored for all these months.

"Well, you told me months ago that you love me. You still do, right? Even though I haven't said the words."

He grinned, the corners of his eyes crinkling. "I know you love me just as much as I love you."

That floored her. "You know?"

"Of course, and so does everyone else." He swooped in and kissed her hard on the mouth, the way he always did before a big decision was made. It had become their trademark Mrs. Garmin had told her a couple of weeks ago.

Elaine groaned. "See, that's the problem. You make it too easy for me. I need to say the words, Liam."

He laughed as Mrs. Garmin appeared around the gate. "Elaine, dear, we need toilet paper and the store is in your shed."

There was never any privacy, she thought with a growl. "Go ahead, Mrs. Garmin. Just make sure you note down how many rolls you're taking." The little woman disappeared, and Elaine grabbed Liam's hand. "Come with me."

Now it was his turn to laugh. "I remember the first time you said that to me."

Memories of that night filtered through her brain and she tugged harder, urging him to a little more speed, because the hit of passion had pleasure spiking through her again. They rushed inside the house.

"Latch the door," she ordered. "Otherwise they'll come looking for us."

At the base of the stairs, their lips met and clung. "I need to shower," he groused. "I'll join you, but first, let me say this. I've been an idiot for months, hiding from the truth. I love you. I love who you are, what you do for everyone. Every day I'm thankful for that chance meeting at the grocery store. I'm thankful for Ramon and everyone around us, but you..." Her eyes burned from unshed tears. "You complete me, Liam. No one else could do that."

"Good then. Now we can make it official."

"What? How are we going to do that?" He shocked her with the ferocity of his demand. "In Scotland they used to marry by making the declaration in front of everyone. I can't think of any people more important than our large community family. Christmas Day, let's make the declaration."

"That's not quite how I imagined it. I wanted flowers and a dress, photographs and—"

"Already taken care of," Liam said with a grin. When she frowned, he slid his hand under her chin. "Mrs. Garmin has been altering her wedding gown for the last month, Ramon has his digital camera, and the flowers? We'll pick them from the gardens you had us plant for the bees."

Just like that, it was planned. "I can't think of anything better."

Liam winked. "Well, there's this one thing. Let's put those pregnancy tests you stashed to good use."

They rushed up the steps to the shower, but only a small portion of their time in there was spent washing. As he lathered her, he whispered encouraging words that heated her from the inside out until she was wanting and starving for his touch.

Lifting her up, he settled her on his very hard cock, sliding in without the barrier she'd come to hate. His skin rubbed against her intimately, and she moved up and down, her body breaking apart with an orgasm that stole her very breath, and he jetted deep within her body.

Afterward, he toweled her down and laid her gently on the bed before climbing in beside her. "I hope that takes, but if it doesn't, we'll try again and again." His hands turned in slow, arousing circles that dipped into every hollow while kissing her, his tongue sliding into her mouth.

Elaine's hands twined in his damp hair as he settled himself once more before sliding home. "Fill me, Liam."

He rocked his hips, nudging at her with exquisite care, one hand cradling her breast. "When you're big and full, your breasts larger than they are now, and I'm inside you, we'll remember this. Me loving you and promising you to be here forever, Elaine. Because I love you."

She moved, suddenly unable to settle for the long, slow loving, and needing him with every ounce of her being.

Liam pounded her, the rhythm wild and hungry, until they exploded in each other's arms.

She lay back, her gaze on the ceiling as he rolled to his side, and she frowned until he returned. "I found this a couple of weeks ago and wondered if you'd wear it for me?"

He produced her grandmother's sapphire and diamond ring, the one that had been removed from her hand only after death. It was a tangible reminder of the longevity of love and the care her grandmother had heaped on her. Tears sprang into her eyes as she remembered the woman who'd given her a childhood of love. And now, the man who offered the ring was offering her the world. It was right.

There was no other answer. "Yes. Yes, I will." They sealed the vow with a kiss.

EPILOGUE

*C*hristmas Day dawned, not with the flurry of presents they'd all experienced themselves, but with an air of festivity nonetheless. In the air, she could smell the cooking meat, and she knew women were out and about gathering foods for their feast.

Today might be a celebration, but they wouldn't forget those they'd lost. Ramon and Liam had taken the largest losses, losing their home, their friends, and contact with anyone they knew before. The death of the phone systems had finalized that. But she'd also lost friends, in Emily and her employer, Mr. Eckerman. They wouldn't ever be forgotten.

Elaine had journaled everything she remembered from the formation of their new community until the present. And each day she added more to it, this wedding being one of the joyous occasions they'd share along with the births and other relationships she was sure would follow them.

Mrs. Garmin stood behind Elaine in the bedroom, fastening the tiny buttons on the gown. "Your grandmother would be so proud of you. Of who you are and what you've become. Of the choices you've made. She'd like Liam too."

They weren't going to have a traditional ceremony, instead deciding they'd meet at the front table and make their declarations, but she couldn't help remembering the old something old—her gown—and something new—their community and family. She touched the earrings in her ears, which were the something borrowed. She didn't forget the something blue either, she thought as he gazed down with misty eyes at her grandmother's sapphire ring on her finger.

She looked back up at Mrs. Garmin. "Would you stand in my grandmother's place and walk me down to meet Liam? It feels right."

Mrs. Garmin sniffed, dabbed at her eyes, and smiled. "I'd be honored."

Ten minutes later, dressed in Mrs. Garmin's gifted gown, she made her way down the stairs with the older woman at her side. Together, hand in hand, they stepped through the garden, past the vegetables, and out into what had been the parklands, now a formal meeting area and growing patch. Their community family waited at the tables. Ramon was there in his jeans and the good shirt they'd hunted down for him, and beyond him, stood Liam. Waiting patiently as he had all these months.

Elaine stopped by his side, and he smiled at her. "I declare before all those gathered that this woman, Elaine, is now my wife. The woman I will love forever."

Someone thrust a hankie into her hand as her vision blurred, and the scent of lavender and roses filled the air. "I declare before our family, here gathered, that this man, Liam, is now my husband. The man I will walk beside for the rest of my life and into eternity."

Amid cheers and whoops they sealed their union with a kiss.

Did you enjoy this book by Imogene Nix?
There's more on the following pages. Just keep turning to see what else.

When Cupid—otherwise known as Diocail— is banished from his home on a remote Scottish Island, he's set a series of tasks by the great god Lugh, who also happens to be his father.

In **Blame The Wine**, he must bring two lovers together... BBW Cara and James, the man she's lusted over from afar who happens to be a super geek and head Veha Industries.

In **A Stranger's Embrace**, Diocail is driven to help an emotionally fragile Jane and Davis, a famous author. The task is more complicated, with the existence of Carstairs her could-be ex-husband and teenage daughter, Frannie.

In **Revenge on Cupid**, Diocail must take the ultimate chance and find his own happily ever after with Simone. Sometimes the past gets in the way and HEA's don't come cheap though.

The dusty, dingy little diner was full, even with its current state of cleanliness—or lack thereof. People from the surrounding offices didn't care about anything except the incredible, well-prepared food at a reasonable cost. They flooded in, like waves to the shore. As one tide left, another swept in.

"Honestly, Simone. I'm going to try getting his attention one more time. If that doesn't work, I'm out of there. I mean, how long can I keep trying?" Cara picked at the caramel tart she hadn't been able to resist with the cheap metal fork and flicked the blob of fresh cream that sat on top to the side of the plate.

"You've said that tons of times before. Besides, what are you going to do to get his attention? Hmm? Walk naked through the typing pool?" Simone bobbed the straw in her smoothie as she eyed her friend with a frown. "It's been what? Eighteen months since you saw him, and you've mooned over him from a distance ever since you met him. You need to move on, Cara. That is, unless there's something you haven't shared?"

The query was arch. Cara shivered even as she shook her head. "No."

Simone quirked an eyebrow, obviously unconvinced with the answer. Cara let out a deep sigh of frustration. "There's a position...it's only temporary, for a PA reporting directly to him." She speared a forkful of tart, chewed quickly and swallowed, before continuing. "In his office, full-time for the period of the engagement. I saw the memo yesterday. I mean, I have the skills, right? I can type, answer phones, make coffee, file, greet people. What's more, I can probably do it better than all those size eights in the typing pool that Ms. Jackman seems to prefer." She nodded thoughtfully. "All I have to do is get past the ogre in Human Resources."

Simone stared at her, disbelief clear on her face. "Girl, I so remember that woman. If you think you can get past her, you're doing better than I ever did. That's why I left Veha Industries, remember? Maybe it's time to haul out your resumé and consider some other options. Look for something better." Simone shook her head and billows of her crimson hair swirled through the still air.

Cara understood Simone only had her best interests at heart. But this time she knew the outcome would be different. Hell, she could feel it in the air. The tingle of expectation.

"Cara, the HR ogre will hang you out for breakfast before she offers you anything like a position in that office. Remember her mantra? Good looks and good work make for a positive workplace!"

Simone didn't sugar-coat anything. It was another great reason for their long- term friendship. Honesty. But Cara didn't want to hear the truth in the statement. Even if it was exactly as her friend said.

Cara nodded quickly. "Yeah, I know, but if I don't try, then I won't know how close I can get to him, right? And the only way to catch his attention is to get past *her* and see him in person." Cara quaked a little at the information she needed to share. The favor she needed to ask. "Anyway, I tidied up my resumé and dropped the application into a memo envelope yesterday, so it's too late to back out now. I mean, fortune favors the brave. Doesn't it? If I don't snag an interview, I'm going to visit the career advisor across the street and register with them." She shrugged. "I'll look for temp work until something more long-term shows up. I can see what they have on offer and well...who knows? Maybe a job with the right boss is just waiting for me. But I'd rather this worked out, to be honest." Her voice trailed off into a whisper. "I really wish he would notice me."

Simone took a long slurp of her banana drink, and Cara noticed her questioning gaze even as she squirmed. Finally, Simone nodded. "It's your funeral. So anyway, you'd better show me this memo if you want me to be a referee for you. I'm guessing that's what you need, right? I'll have to know what I'm supposed to say about you before they ring."

Cara smiled. "Thanks, Simone. I knew I could count on you." She slipped a piece of paper out of her handbag and handed it over. "Sorry it's a bit creased. It was in the bottom of my bag, I stashed it so none of the others from the pool would see. You know how it is."

Available from Love Books Publishing
books2read.com/CelticCupid

Direct Autographed Copy
https://www.imogenenix.net/CelticCupid

STAR OF ISHTAR

Warriors of the Elector
Book One

The first time Elara laid eyes on Grayson was when he rescued her from the clutches of a madman and his scientists who were kidnapping humans and conducting horrific experiments on them. That was years ago. In spite of her attempts to deepen their relationship, they remained nothing more than close friends.Now Elara is a medic with the Admiralty, and she knows what she wants. It's been Grayson since the beginning. When Elara is stationed on the *Star of Ishtar*, she arrives with a plan to further her career. But this time her plan has an added bonus—to finally get her man.

Grayson's spent years fighting the connection between himself and Elara. He's certain it only exist because he saved her life. But his will is failing, and he fears he just might give in to temptation.

"I finally made it." Elara Sudonne watched as the hull of the *Star of Ishtar* loomed in the inky darkness. She clutched her hands tightly together as the shuttle approached the hulking battleship.

This would be her new home and first combat ST placement for the Earth Empire. She quaked inwardly with nerves but fought to keep her serene exterior. Previously her deployments had consisted solely of on-planet expeditions and in rehabilitation and dirtside facilities. When the chance had arisen to move to the battleship, she'd grabbed it with both hands.

The frigid air chilled her bones as she sat in her shuttle seat, but a trickle of sweat inched its way down her back under the fresh gray wool flight uniform. Little puffs of vapor escaped her mouth as she rubbed her arms. Nerves stretched tight, she looked through the small portal at the front of the vessel. She wanted to tug at the collar that somehow seemed to have grown tighter as the ship loomed ahead, but instead she firmed her mouth, straightened her spine, and concentrated on the future.

"So damned long." She'd been working toward this outcome since the day Grayson Myatt and Duvall McCord had saved her from her Ru'Edan captors. She was lucky, she'd survived the 'experimentation' of the Ru'Edan leader Crick Sur Banden's scientists. "And all I have to remind me are my scars." She didn't grin at her own joke.

The person seated behind her jostled but she ignored it, lost in her memories. On that day, so very long ago, the young Elara, fresh-faced and with idealistic views of the empire, was taken from the mall where she'd been shopping with friends, thrust into the back of a transport vehicle, and given to the Ru'Edan scientists to experiment on.

For days they'd worked on her and others, seeking an average pain threshold of humans, slicing her skin then noting reactions and how long it took to heal. They'd cut her arms, body, and even her face, and now she carried the extensive scarring of the exercise as a reminder to herself and others of what they were fighting for. Freedom. The freedom of Earth and its allied planets.

She'd never relinquished hope, it had been her constant companion as she fought against the all-consuming terror. Then they'd found her in that dirty, disused warehouse. They'd found others too, in various states of death and decay. The smells of despair had filled the air with a fetid ripeness that she'd never been able to forget.

Since that day she'd promised herself that she would pay the Ru'Edan back for what they'd done to her. What they'd taken from her. Over the years, she tempered and honed the rage while remaining adamant that she would see the final act played out. She couldn't physically fight, but she had learned about trauma, knew it and understood how it affected a person, and used it as a weapon.

The iron will forged through her experiences had fed her determination, and she'd applied herself to study, finishing in the top ten percent of her class. She entered the medical program at the academy, working hard to excel. Her family remained supportive if perplexed as to why she had chosen to keep reminding herself of what had happened.

The maw of the *Star of Ishtar* loomed closer, opening its cavernous mouth as she watched through the portal. She could hear the voices of the shuttle crew signaling their intention to enter and land, the tinny confirmation coming swiftly. She watched avidly while the shuttle maneuvered, imagining the invisible shields dropping to allow it entry.

Her hands twisted with fear and anger, but she tamped down her emotions. Anger never helped anyone. Staying strong, knowing your history, and ensuring it couldn't be repeated, they were the answers, she told herself firmly, pulling herself from the grip of a dark past so horrific she still saw it in her dreams. She pushed it away to the recesses of her mind and focused on what she was about to do.

A squark overhead, the usual mechanical sound that alerted all on board to a transmission by the captain, caught her attention. "Attention all passengers. We are entering the shuttle bay. Please ensure when you disembark you remove all personal items. Move beyond the white line and wait for your designation."

The lights of the bay flashed as they entered, and once again Elara marveled at how far humanity had moved since they had first walked the Earth. She saw the opening of the structure as the shuttle moved into the bay, inching forward slowly until it stopped its ponderous motion and began its descent to the floor. Something deep inside warmed even as the shuttle's environmental systems began to synchronize with the cooler temperature of the *Star of Ishtar*, and she felt a smile crawl its way over her face.

Elara breathed in deeply, inhaling the metallic-tasting, recycled air and welcoming the calmness that settled on her body. Her eyes closed as she filled her lungs. "I'm here." There was more than a little satisfaction in her tone, and she smiled. She slowly exhaled, finding that center of peace she relied on.

A loud thud and clank echoed as the deep drone split the air. The engines were powering down, and there she was, on one of the Earth Empire's Emeritus class battleships. She sat in her seat, waiting for the all clear from the captain, and once it sounded through the cabin, she rose, tugging at the webbing belt and disengaging it.

The small backpack beside her was all she carried as she made her way to the exit, not needing to duck as so many others did. She stepped through the door, her hands gripping the rail of the cold, metal stairs which connected to the side of the gray shuttle.

She clambered down them slowly, savoring the experience. The sting of the cold on her hands from the stairs, frigid from even their brief exposure to the blackness of space, made her flinch inwardly. The shuttle journey from the Admiralty's strategic base at Aenna to their current position had taken just over an hour, but the whole time it felt like her heart had been in her throat. Her mouth was dry as she followed the new recruits from the ship into the landing bay. She stopped, silently noting the slight mustiness of the air, the recycled quality easily recognizable. Everything, including the oxygen, needed recycling in space.

All around her people swarmed, either around the ships or into the dogleg line that now formed ahead of her. Someone had opened the baggage locker of the shuttle, and the sound of dropping bags hitting the plascrete floor echoed in the air. Another crewmember guided trolleys to the other side of the shuttle, pulling out boxes with important day-to-day items for the ship, including vaccines and plants. She watched briefly, all the while listening to the alien cacophony. Voices called in welcome to old crewmembers, while new ones watched, many goggle-eyed in the fresh uniforms of newly minted officers and crewmembers.

Her gaze flicked around quickly, taking in the sights, sounds, and smells, pungent with oils and grease; burning smells from the scorched plascrete and the press of sweaty or nervous bodies. She joined the line silently, tacking onto the end, and stayed at parade rest, knowing the welcoming voice would cut through the air soon enough. She felt somehow disconnected from the main throng. Perhaps the knowledge that this was the outcome she had worked for years to achieve set her apart. However, still, she felt so...distant from everything around her. She smiled secretly at the bout of whimsy.

"Attention!" The voice boomed out over the plascrete of the docking bay, and she snapped her body into position, noting the commander who had bellowed the words. Technically, she outranked most members aboard the *Star of Ishtar*, except for the command and leadership staff, but she knew all newcomers had to join the welcoming parade, regardless of rank.

Fleet Captain Elphin came into view, his tired features topped by salt-and-pepper gray hair, which highlighted his cool blue eyes. Elara also recognized a body prone to a little middle-aged thickness. Following behind him was his second-in-command, Duvall McCord. A young up-and-coming officer, his status as a fast-tracking officer heading toward his own command, with Elphin both his mentor and captain, had become almost legendary at the academy.

She looked closely at McCord, noting the dynamic drive of his actions and movements. Soon he would achieve a promotion to captain, and she rejoiced for her friend. She'd followed his career with interest and had to tamp down a smile as his eyes betrayed the shock of seeing her before settling into their flat command persona. So he hadn't been apprised of her deployment, she noted, and she had to restrain the tiny feeling of surprise and satisfaction. She filed that snippet of information away.

She caught sight of the man standing behind Duvall. Grayson Myatt. He'd made her heart beat faster for years. Tall and blond with a muscular build and a sexy, tight, little butt, he had pools of deep-blue eyes that had always made her think of forever. He had a growth of stubble on his chiseled jaw, and her fingers itched to touch his perfect lips. Yes, since the day he'd found her in that nasty warehouse tied down like a ragged animal, she'd worshipped him from afar.

Now she had her opportunity to tangle with him, hopefully much closer than any chance that had ever come her way before. With a sigh, she pulled her gaze back to the captain and forced herself to concentrate on his words. She couldn't afford to have her commanding officer angry due to her being distracted.

"Welcome to the *Star of Ishtar*. Most academy recruits want to join us because of what we represent, but on this ship, we only take the best of the best. So, if you made it here, you're the ones we wanted to take a look at. Getting here is only the first step. Staying here is harder to achieve. Our people are the best. Earn your place, and in return, we'll make you one of our crew—a member of the *Star of Ishtar*. Only the best and the brightest wear our uniform and badge. You'll be expected to perform to your absolute limit then give some more. We don't tolerate people who don't pull their weight. Do us proud and wear your uniform with pride." The captain looked out over the new members of his crew. His voice had echoed during his speech, and now it died away.

He scanned the faces before him, and she could almost read his thoughts. There were new security officers and a smattering of other crew. Some of them were young and impressionable, and she knew a few wouldn't make the cut as crewmembers. Others would carve out their place on the *Star of Ishtar* and move to better positions and placements, like she would: the new SurgiTech, a younger female, experienced but untried on board a ship. She smiled at that thought.

Some of those who stood with her would be replaced as they failed the exacting standards the captain set. She'd heard that he was a firm captain, fair but demanding. He'd have to be to command this ship. The Ishtar had well over five hundred at full capacity, and the captain could select their placements as his command staff saw fit from the many who applied to join the crew. She sensed his satisfaction with the choices in the relaxation of his body.

Abruptly, he turned to Duvall, breaking her study of him. "Get them to where they need to present themselves." His words echoed as he walked away. He had a purposeful stride. Quick but unhurried, like he knew where he was going and how to get there. A man who knew how to get what he wanted. Someone to respect and admire.

"My name is Commander Duvall McCord. I am your second-in-command, and my direct subordinate is Commander Grayson Myatt. While you are aboard the *Star of Ishtar* you will be required to fulfill your duties efficiently. As Captain Elphin said, do your job right and you will be one of ours, with all the benefits that come with being a crewmember of the *Star of Ishtar*."

He paused and eyeballed each of the newer recruits, those fresh from the academy. Many of them paled under his gaze, and she smiled inwardly. Even the older people in the line seemed to quake beneath his scowl. He'd always had that air of innate authority, even when barely out of the academy himself. She knew his methods and watched him make full use of the carefully practiced tone of presence.

"Each of you has been assigned. You will present yourselves to the chief of your section. Those details will be found in your orders. Commander Myatt has organized a team to escort you to your cabins. You will have approximately one hour to prepare. We've arranged for crewmembers to escort you to your superiors. Be ready to present for duty. Any issues, you will, of course, take up with your section commander. Should there be need to take any further action, you will see Commander Myatt. You should only see me if you are a command crewmember or as a point of discipline. I am not one for small talk, so if you present to me, have a very good reason."

He delivered the words slowly and deliberately, and Elara restrained a small smile on hearing at least one gulp from those in the line nearest her.

"We run a tight ship here. Discipline and commitment are the two key factors we look for beyond loyalty in our crew. You will from henceforth represent our ship everywhere, and we do not tolerate anything less than the best." He looked around once more, the stern demeanor he wore so well reinforcing the message. If she hadn't known him for so long, she too might have missed the hint of humor glinting in his eyes, the one many took for coldness.

Her legs ached, and she wanted to move and relieve the pressure on them, but she held herself still, waiting for the command to dismiss. She wouldn't let herself or him down now. Not after she'd worked so long to achieve this position.

As the new ST, she had no previous experience on ships. She had vast experience in the field, but Elara was aware that would count for little in the eyes of most of the crew. She didn't intend to signal a weakness to anyone and least of all on her first day aboard the *Star of Ishtar*. That thought held her still and controlled.

She had big shoes to fill after her predecessor, Jamieson, had retired, even though she knew she could fill the void he'd left behind. As a long-term member of the crew—over twenty years—his tenure on the *Star of Ishtar* had placed him aboard since its launch. Due to his experience in the heat of battle with the Ru'Edan he had made a name for himself as the coldest of cold in the hottest of situations.

She hoped to emulate that herself and carve out her own place aboard the Ishtar, as its crew lovingly knew her.

Duvall and Grayson knew how much she wanted to prove herself. They just wouldn't have expected it here, on the Ishtar.

She watched Duvall study her, then, quickly turning on his heel, call to those assembled, "Dismissed."

Once they started to move away, she softened her stance, preparing to turn when the call came.

"Sudonne! A moment if you please."

Elara turned to face Duvall. "Commander?"

"Welcome to the *Star of Ishtar*, Elara. While I am surprised you're the new ST, Grayson and I are pleased you could join us. But how did you manage to pull it off? Keeping it quiet that you were the new ST?" he asked, his voice deep enough to make most women shiver with anticipation.

She smiled, thinking it was a shame she didn't have any feelings for him except sisterly attachment, but then again, given his lack of deep commitment to women, maybe it wasn't such a shame after all.

She understood what drove him. He wanted his own ship and to captain his own future. They'd spent many nights over wine or ale discussing his beliefs that commitment grounded a person. Inwardly, she shrugged. He'd make those calls for himself, though she was sure that one day he would come across someone who would make him consider his choices a little more thoroughly.

"I'm pleased to be here, Duvall. Having an uncle who happens to be an admiral, he was able to let Captain Elphin know that I wanted to surprise you. It's a small world in the Admiralty. Elphin already knew of me, so he okayed my placement. Once the powers knew there was no impediments to me joining the crew, it was fairly simple from there." She felt a small smile creep onto her face, then let it drop away. "What do you think Grayson thinks?"

"Ah, still chasing him, are you?" He grinned, his eyes twinkling. "I think he'll be pleased you're finally old enough and you're here." He looked her straight in the eye. "But you may just need to remind him of that particular fact." He motioned for her to go before him, barking out a deep laugh. "Come on, I'll show you to your cabin."

Available from Love Books Publishing
Available in Ebook via Books2Read

Direct Autographed Copy
https://www.imogenenix.net/Warriors1

THE BLOOD BRIDE BY
IMOGENE NIX

Hope just wants to be an ordinary nestling. She went to college and escaped, but now she's back and there's a secret everyone is keeping from her.

Xavier is the new master of the nest, ready to welcome home the daughter of the house who he has never met. He's unprepared for the woman who steals his breath and enchants him.

Now Hope and Xavier must fight for lives and those of the innocents. After all, it is only by overcoming the rogues that they will have a chance of a timeless future together. But will it be in time?

PROLOGUE

As silence descended on the house, the shadows grew—dark grays and blacks that bled into each other. First one figure then another broke away, making a run toward the house. Silent as the grave, they moved swiftly over dew-slicked grass. Then they stopped still. Waiting. Not a movement betrayed them until a signal propelled them back into action and they started crawling upwards. The walls damp coating no barrier to the intruders that ascended in the darkness.

The sound of each window breaking shattered the quiet—the figures were inside. Screams echoed through the night. Yet, in this area of large estates, heavy with noise-absorbing shrubbery, no one could hear those within. The blood-curdling screams went on and on before finally dying away.

Just one sound echoed through the night: The sobbing of a child.

The front door opened and figures trooped out—ghostly specters against an inky night sky, broken by a single outline. A child in white, carried at the center of the pack.

No sound broke the silence as they moved toward the trees surrounded the house.

Flames now licked at the manor: A deathly glow of oily smoke rising.

All that remained was a single person—wrapped in a cape of midnight blue beyond the house—watching them melt away.

Jemima moved toward the burning structure, breaking into a run as she breached the threshold. Vainly she attempted to enter, but the heat drove her back.

Now dashing tears from her face, she raced across the graveled driveway toward the gates, where the guardhouse was located. No sign of life existed within the building and some instinct of survival slowed her pace to a careful creep. Out of breath and heaving from exertion, she nervously checked within.

Small puffs of white vapor colored the glass. She darted from one window to another. Her cloak drawn tightly around her body, hoping it would camouflage her from sight.

Satisfied, Jemima entered through the heavy, wooden front door and moved toward the phone she spied on the floor. Her eyes darting here and there she dialed, listening to the rotary motor as it returned to the proper position. Time was short and if *they* came back, she needed to have shared the message.

The phone rang once. Twice. With a brrping sound it connected.

"Hello?" A male answered and she felt a warm flush of relief at the voice. A voice she knew well.

"The manor has been breached. The girl child taken." The words erupted and her hand trembled.

"On our way." The click of the receiver being replaced echoed loudly in the stillness of the room.

Copper. She smelled copper.

Her stomach soured, knowing it meant more deaths. Jemima looked around for the gun—a gun with deadly, holy water-infused copper bullets—she knew was hidden somewhere in the room. A gun she couldn't find. *No divine intervention exists here*, she thought.

Hopefully *they* didn't remain. Feeding. If they were still here, that's what they would be doing. She found a corner and scrunched down, hiding from sight.

Crouched low, she tried to stay as still as possible, listening for sounds of the vehicles she knew would be coming. She dug her fingers into the flesh of her arms; remaining aware enough to stop before drawing blood. That would surely bring them out. Jemima dragged the cloak around her to capture the warmth, yet there was little to be found.

The sounds of engines roused her from the corner of the room. Jemima inched toward the window, the lead of the old glass distorting her view, hearing raised voices she knew Mistress Cressida had arrived.

Jemima retreated. Remained hidden from the woman because if she knew, all may well be lost. From the shadowed room she listened to the conversation...

"It smells like Estersham." The Mistress' eyes closed. "If it is, we have a problem." She turned once more, her face set and eyes now glacial in intensity. "James?"

The man nodded as if he knew what was to come.

"If I take those steps, I cannot return. Another must stand in my place." Her voice hardened while her eyes glittered in the dim light, piercing in their intensity.

Then the Mistress' voice called out in the near silence. "You and yours have been my loyal servants for so many years. I took an oath to protect you long ago. I renewed it with marriage and births, over and over. Now, my home and yours have been breached and this child taken from us. The girl child, who will be the hope and salvation of our kind, was ripped from the bosom of our nest. I will repay your loyalty and I will get her back." The words of power rippled in the night and licked at Jemima's skin.

Available in Ebook
books2read.com/BloodBride-Nix

Direct Autographed Copy
https://www.imogenenix.net/BloodBride

ALSO BY IMOGENE NIX

<u>Warriors of the Elector</u>

- Star of Ishtar
- Starline
- Starfire
- Star of the Fleet
- Starburst
- The Star of Eternity

The Star of Ishtar & Starline - Print

Starfire & Star of the Fleet - Print

Starburst & The Star of Eternity - Print

<u>Blood Secrets</u>

- The Blood Bride
- The Illuminated Witch
- The Sorcerer's Touch

The Secrets World:

<u>Blood Secrets</u>

- The Blood Bride
- The Illuminated Witch
- The Sorcerer's Touch

<u>House Secrets</u>

- As Dawn Breaks
- Immortal Consequences
- Unnamed Book III

All That Glitters - a House Secrets Novella (Coming in 2023)

<u>Danu's Secrets</u>

- The Downfall of Padraic O'Shaunessy (Coming in 2023)
- Unnamed Secrets Book II

<u>The Automaton Series</u>

- Haven House (Coming 2022)
- Nobel Crest (Coming 2022)

<u>The Search Duology</u>

- Miss Elspeth's Desire
- Miss Isabelle's Craving

<u>Reunion Trilogy</u>

- War's End
- The Assassin
- Executing Justice

The Reunion Trilogy in Paperback

<u>Sex Love & Aliens</u>

- Tangled Webs
- False Webs
- Covert Webs

21st Testing Protocol

- Cyborg: Redux
- Children Of A Greater Evil
- When Evil Came To Stay
- Finis: The War To End All Wars

Celtic Cupid Trilogy

- Blame The Wine
- A Stranger's Embrace
- Revenge On Cupid

The Celtic Cupid Trilogy in Paperback

Zombieology

- The Reset
- I Dream of Zombies
- The Six Million Dollar Zombie
- Make Room For Zombies (2022)
- Unnamed Zombiology Book (coming 2023)

Knights of Pleasure

- Silken Knights (Coming in September 2022)

Single Titles

The Chocolate Affair (also in Print)

Falling In Love Again (Previously A Sapphire For Karina)

BioCybe (also in Print)

Hesparia's Tears (also in Print)

Tomorrow's Promise

A Bar In Paris (also in Print)

Inheritance Of The Blood (also in Print)

The Plan

Loving Memories (also in Print)

Hero of Heartbreak Hill (also in Print)

My One & Only

Curse Bound (coming 2021)

Raspberry Dreams (Not Yet Released)

Non Fiction

Self Publishing: Absolute Beginners Guide (With Suzi Love)

Written as Ciara Cave

25 Curated Ways To Get Rid Of Telemarketers

Book Signings for Absolute Beginners

ABOUT THE AUTHOR

Imogene is published in a range of romance genres including Paranormal, Science Fiction and Contemporary. She is mainly published in the UK and USA.

In 2010, Imogene Nix (the pen name not Imogene herself) was born. Imogene sat down and worked tirelessly for 3 months culminating in the book Starline, which became the first in a trilogy titled, "Warriors of the Elector." Since then she's had over 30 titles published and is now focusing on hybridising herself - with a mixture of traditionally published and self-published works.

In fact, she's taking control of many of her back catalogue books, which are slowly re-releasing as self-published titles.

Imogene is a member of a range of professional organisations world wide, and believes in the mantra of mentoring and paying it forward and is actively involved in mentorship (through NaNoWrimo and her vlog: In The Chair With Imogene Nix) and tutoring of new and upcoming authors.

In her spare time she loves to drink coffee, wine & eat chocolate and is parenting more than one spoilt cat along with her husband and daughters and looks forward to weekends away with her husband in their caravan "The Seven Year Hitch!" Do look forward to her caravan romance at some point!

To Contact Imogene

www.imogenenix.net
imogene@imogenenix.net

facebook.com/ImogeneNix
twitter.com/ImogeneNix
instagram.com/ImogeneNix
bookbub.com/authors/imogenenix